Maria's
Italian Spring

Also by Gillian Avery

Maria Escapes

Trespassers at Charlcote

James without Thomas

The Elephant War

To Tame a Sister

The Greatest Gresham

The Peacock House

Call of the Valley

Maria's Italian Spring

Gillian Avery

illustrated by
Scott Snow

Simon & Schuster Books for Young Readers

Published by Simon & Schuster
New York   London   Toronto   Sydney   Tokyo   Singapore

SIMON & SCHUSTER
BOOKS FOR YOUNG READERS
Simon & Schuster Building, Rockefeller Center
1230 Avenue of the Americas
New York, New York 10020

10   9   8   7   6   5   4   3   2   1

Library of Congress Cataloging-in-Publication Data
Avery, Gillian [Italian spring] Maria's Italian spring / by Gillian Avery ;
illustrated by Scott Snow.   p.   cm.
Previously published as: The Italian spring.
Summary: When her latest guardian dies, a twelve-year-old
English girl is relieved when a distant cousin offers her
a home in Italy.
[1. Orphans—Fiction. 2. Italy—Fiction.] I. Snow, Scott, ill.
II. Title. PZ7.A939Mat 1993 [Fic]—dc20 92–16955 CIP
ISBN: 0–671–79582–1

Contents

Maria Alone

The Reverend Henry Henniker-Hadden, warden of Canterbury College, Oxford, great-uncle and guardian of Maria Henniker-Hadden, died on February 15, 1877. On that day Maria was left alone in the world. There was nobody left at all. Her parents had died in India when she was a few months old, and all her childhood had been spent in Bath with her mother's aunt. There had been a brief and miserable period at Semphill House, a girls' school in the Midlands, just before Great-Aunt Lucia's death, and then in May 1875 she had gone to live with Uncle Hadden at Oxford. It had been a happy arrangement, they had enjoyed each other's company, and Uncle Hadden had taught Maria himself in the somber library of the Lodgings at Canterbury College, where the walls were lined from ceiling to floor with brown calf-bound books.

But it had lasted so short a time, hardly two years. Uncle Hadden had not seemed ill. He was old perhaps, and a little slow in his movements, but as well as his duties as warden of the college, he had still found time to do a great deal of reading, and to give Maria two hours' teaching a day, doing a little in the way of Euclid and arithmetic, and reading Greek and Latin with her, for he said he saw the makings of a classical scholar in her. She used to work by herself the rest of the time, but she loved it. She liked being by herself, having the freedom of her uncle's library, and above all being in Oxford.

She had not bothered to think of the future. The days glided past so peacefully, so uneventfully, it never crossed her mind that they would not continue to do so forever and ever. But then she had walked into the library that February evening to say good night. Uncle Hadden was sitting in his armchair as usual, but there was something about his stillness that had sent her running, crying, for Mrs. Clomper in the housekeeper's room.

She saw her uncle once again. Mrs. Clomper, with much rustling of black bombazine, had led her by the hand to the library, and there lay Uncle Hadden in his coffin. (Maria had never been close to a coffin before; she never knew they were so magnificent, so highly polished, so richly lined.) She had hardly recognized Uncle Hadden, his face was so still and waxen. Obediently, following Mrs. Clomper's example; she sunk to her knees, rose after a moment, and then was led out.

She did not go to the funeral, of course; only gentlemen went to that. She did not even peep out through the drawn curtains when she heard the solemn sound of slow footsteps tramping out of the house into the quadrangle, pacing over the flagstones, as Uncle Hadden was carried to the chapel. All the time the bell tolled, a deep note that echoed quiveringly around the quad, thirty seconds and then another—dong. Maria wondered how it was done, whether the bellringer counted, or whether he had a clock to time his strokes. Then the tolling stopped, and she parted the curtains, and listened. After a while she heard, carried on a gust of wind, the choir singing. She remembered the last time she heard the choir—in chapel, last Sunday with Uncle Hadden sitting a few yards away in the warden's stall. He would never sit there again. Maria wept, sitting on the window seat in her black dress.

People had been very kind. Mrs. Smith, whom she knew from the brief time she had shared lessons with the Smith boys when she first arrived in Oxford, came to fetch her and carried her off to spend the day. But the three Smith boys were all at school now, and it was embarrassing to have so much grown-up attention focused on her. Professor Smith had always rather frightened her; he teased so, and she could never be certain how much was teasing and how much was serious. Then when Joshua and James had come back from school in the afternoon they had eyed her nervously as though she had suddenly turned into a new sort of person. Even James, so bumptious and bouncing, had been subdued, and they had all played Snakes and Ladders in a polite and strained way that seemed thoroughly unnatural.

Left to herself in the Lodgings, she just wandered around miserably. She could not go out, for there was no one to take her, and besides, it was February and the weather hardly tempted one outside. Rain poured down, bouncing up from the flagstones of the quad, and pattering on the windowpanes. There was no point in working, for who would look over her exercises? She did not like to go into the library; it seemed a place set apart now that Uncle Hadden had died there. So she sat in the rather gloomy room that had been given up to her as a sitting room, and played endless games of solitaire on the board that Uncle Hadden had used when he was a boy.

Mrs. Clomper, the housekeeper, was in charge of her, of course, but she was deeply occupied these days. Maria knew enough to realize that she could not stay in the Lodgings very much longer. The college would elect a new warden, who would move into the house.

They might have elected one already for all she knew, somebody who was waiting impatiently until he could put his own belongings where Uncle Hadden's had been. Whatever it was, Mrs. Clomper was busy counting linen, turning out the silver and plate, going through lists and inventories with clerks and people who always seemed to be around the house.

"Rushed off my feet, not a moment to myself," she said to Maria over one of the hurried meals that they had together in the housekeeper's room. She was not bad tempered as Maria had sometimes known her, just "rushed," as she said, and Maria did not dare ask her the question that tormented her all the time: "What is going to become of me?" Mrs. Clomper, she told herself, was too busy for such questions. The fact was, Maria was frightened of the answer. She could not imagine what would become of her, for there was no one left, no one at all. There were people who looked after her affairs, lawyers in London, but nobody with whom she could live.

In the end she did ask Mrs. Clomper. She had been lying awake worrying, and she felt she could bear it no longer. It was about a week after the funeral. Mrs. Clomper had been particularly late for lunch, and Maria had sat there, staring at the lamb cutlets that were lying in congealing gravy. She was not particularly impatient to start her meal, but she would have preferred to eat the cutlets before the gravy had turned into a white crust. Then, at last, Mrs. Clomper had hurried in.

"I'm sorry to keep you waiting, Miss Maria, I'm sure, but it's nothing but rush, hurry, scurry all day long, and having to stop what I'm doing all the time because of gentlemen from Mr. Furnivall's office, and the college bursar, and goodness knows who else. And Mr. Burghclere in Italy and us trying to do all the arranging without him."

"Who is Mr. Burghclere?" asked Maria apprehensively. Perhaps he was the person who was going to take charge of her.

"Mr. Burghclere? Why, fancy you not knowing who he is. Though, come to think of it, I suppose you might not know the name, seeing it's the other side of the family and a distant enough connection at that. Mr. John Burghclere is the poor warden's cousin, though not a near cousin, and he's the one who's going to have all the warden's books and that."

"Is he the person who's going to look after me?" said Maria in a small voice. She felt as though cold water were trickling down her back, down her arms and legs, as she sat shivering, waiting for Mrs. Clomper's answer. She would know now, for better or for worse, what her fate was going to be.

"Look after you?" Mrs. Clomper seemed very startled. "Certainly not, Miss Maria, he's not that sort of gentleman at all. Very bookish he is, travels a lot, writes things in the papers. Besides, he hasn't got a house of his own, not what you'd call an establishment. There's this villa he lives in in Italy, and when he's in London he's got chambers in Albany. No, it's no good you getting ideas in that direction, Miss Maria. You'll be going off to school as soon as the lawyers have made up their minds what school it's to be."

Maria stared at her, appalled. "Do you think it would be Semphill House?" Of course, school had been at the back of her mind all the time, but she had never dared bring the thought into the open.

"It might be. Who am I to say? Now, eat that cutlet up, Miss Maria, there's a good girl. We've dillydallied over this lunch enough as it is, and they'll be wanting to get on in the kitchen."

But Maria pushed the plate away from her untasted. She felt sick, she could not possibly eat it, and all Mrs. Clomper's urgings had no effect. Eventually she burst into tears and ran out of the room. An hour later she was still crying, hysterically now, unable to stop, gasping for breath, wheezing like broken bellows. Mrs. Clomper had come in once or twice to see how she was, and the last time she spoke to her severely.

"Now, stop it, Miss Maria, this instant, or you'll cry yourself into a fit. There's nothing wrong with school.

There's many a girl who'd be glad of your chances in life."

"I can't stop," gasped Maria, herself frightened by the ferocity of her weeping. "And I think I'm going to be sick."

An hour later Dr. Jessop came. Maria was in bed by this time. She was still shaking all over from her crying fit, and she felt very cold and sick. She hardly knew Dr. Jessop, she was aware of him as a jolly, kindly sort of man who did not drive in a brougham like most doctors, but dashed about Oxford in a smart dogcart with a dalmatian trotting behind. She had seen him going into the Smiths' house when one of the boys was ill. She had also met him when, on one occasion, she had gone to tea with his daughter. She had liked him then; he was cheerful and easy-mannered, and when he teased he teased in a way one could understand, unlike Professor Smith.

On this occasion he was sympathetic. "Been crying, eh? Well, you've had a lot to put up with, so we can't really blame you, but whatever these lady novelists tell you, crying doesn't really help. Now, what does help is having your mind taken off things, so why don't you come and have tea tomorrow with my little Hetty. She's the only child in the house, and she gets lonely. It's Saturday tomorrow, so she'll be home from school. I tell you what, I'll call round in the afternoon to make sure you're fit to go out, and if you are, we'll wrap you up warmly and carry you back in the dogcart. Ever driven in a dogcart? No? Well, there's a treat in store for you. It's the smartest turnout in Oxford, though I say it myself, and you should see my Fairy running after it. If ever there was a good dog, it's Fairy."

Maria was not certain that she really wanted to be well enough to go out the following afternoon. She knew Harriet Jessop slightly. Harriet had been asked to the Lodgings to meet her, and Maria had made a return visit to the Jessops' house in north Oxford, but the two girls had not found much to say to each other, and it had been a relief on both occasions when their maids had come to fetch them away. Besides, Maria disliked girls on principle. She had led a very secluded life while with her great-aunt and had met very few children of her own age. During her few weeks at Semphill House she had decided that her companions were unbearably stupid with their giggling and chatter, and unkind and mean-spirited as well. And Thomas, Joshua, and James Smith, with whom she had done lessons for a month or two the previous summer, had encouraged her to despise the female species. They also had a very low opinion of Harriet Jessop.

But when Dr. Jessop came on Saturday, he said Maria was quite fit for the drive, and well muffled up in scarves, a shawl, and a sealskin muff that Mrs. Clomper lent her, to say nothing of the plaid rugs Dr. Jessop put around her, she mounted the dogcart and was driven through the streets of Oxford. Up the Cornmarket, St. Giles, and the Banbury road toward the Jessops' house in Bradmore Road. It was not actually raining, though damp was in the air. The rawness whipped pink into Maria's cheeks, and she thought it was very pleasant to be driving uncovered like this; she wished it could go on forever, and that she did not have to face Harriet. It was so easy to make conversation with Dr. Jessop, but she knew she would feel ill at ease with his daughter. She never knew what to say to girls.

But Bradmore Road was no distance from the town, a road of forbidding yellow-brick houses with windows more suitable for a church than a home. Dr. Jessop pulled up outside one of them, jumped down, and then helped Maria from her seat. Pat, the Irish groom, held the horse.

"There's my little Hetty at the dining room window, waiting for us," he said, pointing. "See that tiny corner of the curtain pulled away? That's my Hetty. Just like the people who draw their curtains for funerals but can't help having a bit of a look all the same." He waved vigorously. "All right, Hetty, we'll be in in a trice."

The crack in the lace curtains disappeared. Fairy the dalmatian bounded up the steps in front of them and sat on the top one, thumping her tail. Dr. Jessop rang, and a parlor maid appeared.

"I can see you, Hetty, peering round the dining room door," bellowed Dr. Jessop cheerfully. "Come along, then."

Rather timidly and smiling nervously, Harriet came down the hall toward them. She was a tall, clumsy sort of girl who always seemed to be stooping to try to make herself smaller, and to have immense difficulty in managing her hands and feet. She shook Maria's hand with one that was large and cold and red-knuckled, and then stood there watching uneasily as Dr. Jessop helped Maria off with her wraps. This done, Dr. Jessop rumpled Harriet's hair affectionately, drew her to him, and gave her a smacking kiss.

"Well, she's here at last. Too excited to eat any lunch, weren't you, Hetty? Where's your mother? What are you two little lasses going to do with yourselves this afternoon?"

"Mother's in the drawing room doing the Working Girls' Guild accounts. She's had a fire lit for us in the dining room, so we're going to be there."

A door opened farther down the hall, and Mrs. Jessop appeared. She was a bony, angular woman who devoted a great deal of time, as Maria remembered her, to committees and good works, and who seemed rather remote from her family and from Harriet and her affairs in particular. Not that Maria had minded this; she always felt ill at ease if people took too much notice of her. But Mrs. Jessop's cool manner seemed to make

Harriet more awkward and clumsy than ever. At this moment Mrs. Jessop was holding a sheet of paper in her hand which she scanned as she walked up toward them.

"Good afternoon, Maria. It is very nice of you to come and take tea with Harriet. She has been begging to see you. Now, there's a nice fire lit for you two girls in the dining room. Suppose you run along there."

"We don't often have fires here," said Harriet nervously as she held the dining room door open for Maria. "It's because of you coming."

But in spite of the fire the room seemed very cold. It was a dark place, with a huge table of black wood, and chairs covered with black horsehair ranged stiffly down either side. On the table, arranged very neatly, was a collection of small china dolls. There was also a work box and a few pieces of material.

"I thought perhaps we could make clothes for these dolls," said Harriet with a sort of a gasp. "They haven't got any."

Maria had never been a doll-playing sort of child. She might have had them when she was a baby, but never since she could remember, and besides, once she became acquainted with the Smith boys, she had been taught to have a horror of girl occupations. Harriet must have sensed her hesitation.

"Or don't you like dolls?" she added nervously.

"I don't know much about them, I'm afraid." Maria

picked up one. It stared back at her with a stiff smile on its painted face. "But I expect I could help you sew some clothes, though I'm not very good at sewing."

"Oh, *I* don't want clothes for them," said Harriet hastily. "It's just that I thought you might like doing it. And Mother will be glad. She thinks it's dreadful to care about dolls when there are real babies and children that need clothes sewn for them." She swept the dolls up into a bundle. "What would you like to do, then?"

"I don't mind at all," said Maria politely.

"Would you like to see my books? I haven't got many though, and I expect you've got hundreds."

"Not many of my own. Uncle Hadden had so many, and I was always allowed to take what I wanted from the library." Maria stopped. She remembered again the last occasion that she was in the library.

Mention of Uncle Hadden clearly had a most unnerving effect on Harriet. She ran on like a runaway horse, trying to bolt from the unpleasant subject of Maria's bereavement. "Papa's got some books in the study, but medical ones, I think, and Mother mostly reads books about political science and prison reform and women's rights. She's terribly interested in prisoners' babies and women's rights. I'm not, though I address envelopes for her sometimes and make clothes for the babies. I like storybooks best, though Mother says it's self-indulgent to read them and I'm never allowed to read them in the mornings. Do you read storybooks?"

Maria felt rather dazed by all this chatter. "Sometimes I read Scott. And Joshua Smith lent me some boys' books—Captain Marryat and Captain Mayne Reid."

"Oh, I see, I don't know anything about those. But if you want to read storybooks I can lend you good ones like *Jessica's First Prayer* and *Little Meg's Children*, which are dreadfully sad. Do you know them? Oh, I forgot, you probably read very clever things, not storybooks at all. Papa says you know Greek and Latin even though you're only twelve. Who taught you? You didn't go to school, did you?"

"I did lessons for a little while with some boys, and then Uncle Hadden taught me," said Maria.

Harriet gave another gasp. She had gotten near dangerous ground again. "They do Greek and Latin at my school, the Oxford Ladies' College. At least, the clever ones do. It's quite a good school. Four of our old girls are lady students at the university now, and they say that probably Beatrice Haddow will be next year and perhaps Ethel Whitehead will try to be a lady doctor. Just fancy, a lady doctor. Would you like to be a lady doctor?"

Maria shook her head. Last May she had told Uncle Hadden that more than anything she wanted to be a professor of Greek. He had not laughed at her; he had treated it seriously. But he was the only person she could ever talk to about it; there would never be anybody else. Feeling tears coming into her eyes, she walked to the windows and peered out. There was nothing interesting to be seen in Bradmore Road, just another yellow-brick house exactly like the Jessops' house, with a flight of stone steps leading up to its front door, and a meager patch of front yard. But Maria stood and stared, and after a while Harriet came timidly over and stared out too. She seemed to feel as hostess that it was her duty to make conversation however disinclined Maria was for it, so after a minute or two of agitated silence when she was all too obviously beating her brains for something to say, she started again.

"Our school is really quite a good school. I mean, clever people's children go there; some of their fathers are professors, even. Do you think you'll ever go to it?" She paused, and then added in a rush, very boldly, "It would be so nice if you did someday. I mean, we're the same age and we might be in the same class and it would be so nice to have a proper friend."

She stopped, very red. The embarrassed Maria had no chance of replying, which was fortunate, as she had no idea what to say, for at that moment the door was thrown open and Fairy came lumbering in, followed by Dr. Jessop.

" 'Nice to have a proper friend,' eh, Hetty? What's all this about?" ·

Harriet blushed redder than ever. "I was just saying that it would be nice if Maria could come to my school, Papa. I mean, it is quite a good school, isn't it? For clever people?"

"Oh, yes, it's clever enough, certainly. That's why your mother chose it, so that you could have a chance of being an independent woman. Though why women should want to be independent beats me, especially nice, clinging little creatures like you, Hetty."

"I don't want to be independent, Papa."

"That's my girl. Well, come along, you two young creatures. Polly has taken tea into the sitting room."

If Harriet had seemed confused and embarrassed alone with Maria in the sitting room, in front of her mother she was a thousand times worse. She appeared quite unused to drawing room tea, and having to balance a plate in one hand and a cup and saucer in the other. She slopped tea into her saucer and dropped crumbs on the carpet; she knocked over the milk jug, and spent a lot of the time with a hot face, groping around on the floor for the things she had let fall. Mrs. Jessop said very little, though she sighed over Harriet's worst clumsinesses, and Maria said nothing at all, except to reply to such questions as were asked of her. The only person who seemed to be enjoying himself was Dr. Jessop. He

lay stretched out in an enormous armchair, the dalmatian lying heavily across his feet, and drank his tea out of the largest cup Maria had ever seen. It even had a sort of ledge across the top to rest his whiskers upon.

"That's better, upon my word," he said after his fourth cup. "The world couldn't go round without tea. The wonder is that it manages to go round at all between lunch and tea time. Hetty, your mother seems very abstracted."

"It's the accounts for the Working Girls," said Mrs. Jessop with her forehead creased. "They don't make any sense at all. I can see that I shall have to go right through the books tonight, and that means another evening wasted. The incompetence of most people is really unbelievable."

"If I were you," said Dr. Jessop, turning to Harriet and Maria, "I should stay out of this sort of business altogether. You'll either spend your time making mistakes, or else you'll have to unravel other people's. Just stay at home and sew a fine seam, that's the best thing."

"Harriet, alas, cannot even sew a fine seam," said Mrs. Jessop dampingly.

Dr. Jessop took Maria home soon after that. Even though she was only going back to Mrs. Clomper and the cold, empty Lodgings, Maria was glad to escape. Harriet seemed very sorry to see her go, and looked at her beseechingly when Mrs. Jessop said that she hoped

Maria would come again soon. But Maria could only think what a relief it was not to have to wonder what to say to her.

"It would be nice for Hetty if they did send you to the Ladies' College," said Dr. Jessop reflectively as they drove back. "She's a bit lonely, poor little thing, doesn't seem to make friends easily, and I should say you would be just the girl for her."

Maria received this in silence. The Oxford Ladies' College sounded as much of a prison as Semphill House, and she could not think she and Harriet could ever be friends. If you cannot even talk to a person, how can you possibly be friendly with her?

"Don't you want to go to school, then?" said Dr. Jessop, looking over his shoulder at her. "Have you ever been at one? They're not as bad as all that."

"Semphill House was *horrible*," said Maria in a trembling voice.

"Not all schools are good, of course." Dr. Jessop turned the mare down Canterbury Lane. "Some of them I wouldn't choose to send a girl to. But for a clever girl—and by all accounts you're a clever girl—Oxford Ladies' College isn't at all bad, you know. Well, here we are. I hope they let us know how things go with you. And if there's anything we can ever do for you, tell us."

He helped Maria down, stood waiting until the maid had opened the door for her, and then with a wave of his hand he got back into the dogcart. Through the closed door she heard the mare clip-clopping up the lane, and she felt suddenly that the only person in the world who was kind to her had gone forever.

School

*S*o the visit to the Jessops hardly helped Maria to forget her troubles. Indeed, it made her rather more aware of them, for after her conversation with Dr. Jessop she began to realize that school was inevitable. What else could people do with her? There was nobody left who could give her a home. In fact, it was not just a question of school for nine months of the twelve, it would be school during the holidays too, like poor Alice at Semphill House, whose parents were in India. And Maria remembered with deep despair how downtrodden and timid Alice always seemed.

Mrs. Clomper knew no more than Maria, and being very busy clearing up the Lodgings, she gave the matter rather less thought. Once or twice she did say, more to herself than to Maria, that she hoped the business would be settled soon, all this hanging around made it very difficult for a body to make plans. Maria felt sure that "this business" was in fact herself, and she flinched. She did not know which she hated most, the uncertainty (this was horrible, but at least nothing had actually happened yet), or the thought of the final decision. The uncertainty was not to last much longer. Two or three days after the visit to Bradmore Road, Mrs. Clomper announced over breakfast that she had heard from "the gentlemen in London," that she was to take Maria to see them the next day, and she hoped to goodness something was decided then. She could not bear this waiting much longer.

Maria had never been to London properly before. She had driven across it last summer with Uncle Hadden, between Paddington and Charing Cross, and that was all. Setting off from Oxford station this raw February day, she thought it was rather sad that an expedition that should have been so exciting was spoiled by having to wonder nervously what the lawyers were going to say to her, what the final, irrevocable decision was going to be. Mrs. Clomper slept all the way. She loosened her coat, untied the strings of her bonnet, shut her eyes, and did not open them until the train steamed into Paddington. Maria just gazed out of the window of their second-class compartment and looked at the dark, wintry fields that were rushing by, wondering whether there was anything she could say to the lawyers to persuade them not to send her to school.

At Paddington Mrs. Clomper roused herself with much energy, tied her bonnet strings, and descended very purposefully onto the platform. She waved fiercely at a porter with her umbrella, commanded him to fetch them a four-wheeler, and to "look sharp about it, the young lady has an appointment in the Temple in half an hour." When the four-wheeler lumbered up, Mrs. Clomper gave the porter a sharp look, put tuppence into his hand, and having seen Maria into the growler, clambered in behind her. Maria stared out through the dirty windows. Every second, every step, was taking her nearer the lawyers' decision about her future. Why couldn't the cab go on forever? The route was very much the same as it had been to Charing Cross last summer, through Hyde Park, now bare and leafless. There were no elegant ladies in open carriages, no people riding or strolling in the park; the few pedestrians that they saw were in a hurry to escape from the bleak east wind. The cab went past Charing Cross, and down the crowded Strand, where progress was very much slower. At last it turned off, under an archway, and left the jostle of the Strand for the quiet of the Temple. There, in a square surrounded by dignified red-brick buildings with deep windows, the cab stopped. Mrs.

Clomper looked no less in command of the situation than she had been at Paddington. With her umbrella gripped as though it were a weapon, she stalked through the black door of No. 19 New Court, followed by the shrinking Maria. They found themselves in an office stacked from floor to ceiling with enormous ledgers and black tin boxes. The rest of the space was taken up by four very high desks at which sat two elderly men and two young ones on high stools. Mrs. Clomper rapped on the floor with her umbrella.

"This young lady has an appointment to see Mr. Josephs at twelve o'clock. It is twelve o'clock now," she said accusingly.

They were ushered into a little inner room that was also lined with black tin boxes. There were two leather armchairs. Mrs. Clomper seated herself on one and gestured to Maria to sit down on the other. Maria sat on the very edge, listening apprehensively to the tramp of feet mounting the stairs and then walking over the floor above their heads. At this very minute they're telling Mr. Josephs I'm here, she thought. Even if I ran out at once I couldn't escape.

Presently the footsteps recrossed the floor above, came down the stairs, and approached the door of the room where Maria and Mrs. Clomper were sitting. One of the young clerks put his head around the door.

"Mr. Josephs will see the young lady now," he said,

and held a door open for them to pass through. They went up a dark staircase where the walls were so blackened with London soot that you could not tell what color they had once been painted. They were shown into a room at the top. It had a smell that was familiar to Maria, the smell of the library at the Lodgings, of moldering leather bindings. Like the library, the walls of this room were bookshelves full of brown leather books. A fire burned brightly in the carved wood chimneypiece, and in front of it stooped Mr. Josephs, slowly rubbing his hands together. Maria had never seen him before. During Aunt Lucia's and Uncle Hadden's lifetime this had not been necessary. He did not look unkind, Maria thought, giving him a frightened look; just rather gray and wrinkled and remote. When she had shaken hands with him she sat down on the edge of a leather chair with wooden arms and stared out of the window at the bare branches of a plane tree outside. Mr. Josephs was talking to Mrs. Clomper.

"The letter that you forwarded to me," he was saying, "was from a Dr. Jessop. You know him? He had a suggestion to make as regards the future of our young friend here. If it is decided to send her to school, he offers her a home with his own family. From there she could attend a day school in Oxford. Or alternatively, she could go to boarding school and spend the holidays with Mrs. Jessop and himself."

Maria took her eyes off the bare twigs outside and stared stupefied at Mr. Josephs, who had now gone over to his desk and was looking through papers on it. "Here is the letter," he said, putting on some gold-rimmed spectacles. "Let us see what Dr. Jessop says. Ah, yes. 'The arrangement which would undoubtedly please us most would be for the child to attend the same school as our own daughter, the Oxford Ladies' College, as a day student, for in that case we could have her with us the whole time. But if it is decided to send her to boarding school, we should be delighted for her to make her home with us in the holidays.'" Mr. Josephs laid the letter on his desk. "We would have to investigate the matter a little further, of course. But on the whole it seems an excellent idea. And what does our young friend think of it?" He turned to Maria, rubbing his hands around each other.

"I don't know," said Maria dully, knowing very well that she hated the idea.

"You would prefer to go to boarding school?" persisted Mr. Josephs.

Maria, feeling that she was being harried by horrible logical arguments when all the time she just wanted to tell somebody how miserable she was and how she hated the idea of boarding school and day school equally, just shook her head dumbly.

"No, I don't somehow think that boarding school

would be a very good idea," said Mr. Josephs, looking thoughtfully at Maria under large gray eyebrows. "I seem to remember that your last experience of boarding school was not happy. I think, then, we shall give Dr. Jessop's suggestion a trial. Any arrangement that we make for you is bound to seem strange at first, but I am sure you will settle down soon."

And that was that. There was a certain amount of conferring and discussion of various matters between Mrs. Clomper and Mr. Josephs, but nothing that Maria took any part in. She just sat in her chair, staring out at the branches of the plane tree against the dull white sky, fixing the shape of the tree in her mind so that she was never able to forget it, and always, in later years, when anybody spoke of "school" she would instantly see that wintry sky and the black pattern of twigs against it. She shook hands limply with Mr. Josephs ten minutes later, and for the whole of the journey back—in the cab to Paddington, their lunch in the buffet at the station, the two hours in the train to Oxford—she kept her eyes fixed rigidly on a point a few inches over Mrs. Clomper's head, afraid that if she relaxed at all, the tears would start pouring down her face.

The arrangements for her to start at the Oxford Ladies' College went forward very rapidly. Dr. Jessop undertook them, and he was very kind. He called in at the Lodgings nearly every day to discuss things with Mrs. Clomper, and finally he took Maria to see Miss Raby, the headmistress, herself. Maria was limp with fright on that occasion, and Miss Raby, tall and forbidding with pince-nez that were attached by a sort of gold spring to a clip on her bodice, did nothing to help her over her fears. Dr. Jessop did all the talking. He told Miss Raby, who seemed to eye Maria like a farmer assessing an animal he is undecided whether to buy, how advanced Maria was in her studies. Then later on, as they drove back to the Lodgings together, Dr. Jessop talked about Miss Raby.

"Formidable female, that. Though she's kind enough to Hetty, got a soft spot for her, you might almost say, if a gorgon like that could be soft in any spot. Hetty likes her too. But these bluestockings aren't for me, though I mustn't say too much in case you turn out to be one. Now, when are we going to see you in Bradmore Road?"

It was fixed with Mrs. Clomper that Maria should be moved to Bradmore Road on Friday, so that she could start school the following Monday. Maria listened silently while all this was discussed, then as soon as Dr. Jessop had gone, she flung herself into the startled Mrs. Clomper's arms.

"Let me stay here," she sobbed. "I'll be good, really I will. I won't get in anybody's way. But let me be here and not with the Jessops."

Mrs. Clomper was startled. She also seemed quite touched. Maria had never shown her any affection before. "It's not that you get in the way, Miss Maria, there hardly could be a quieter little thing, as I've said often enough to Cook since the poor warden went. It's just that all the servants will be gone after the end of the week, and I'm staying on only till Mr. Burghclere's been here and settled things, which I expect will be very soon now, as I've had a letter from him saying that he is arriving in England on the twenty-seventh. The Lodgings is no place for a young lady like you, everything higgledy-piggledy and no comfort anywhere, no regular meals after this week either. Dr. Jessop's such a kindly gentleman, you'll be far better off with him and his little girl."

"But I know it here, I like it," sobbed Maria. "I don't mind if there aren't regular meals. Please, Mrs. Clomper, do let me stay. It's bad enough going to school where I won't know anybody, without having to go to a house where I don't know the people."

In the end Mrs. Clomper gave way. "You can stay for a bit longer, then, though I don't see what difference a few days is going to make to you. Till Mr. Burghclere comes, of course. After that I won't be here myself, I'm only waiting to see what he wants done about the books and all, and then I'm off to my sister and her husband at Banbury."

Maria grasped at this reprieve with both hands. If only she could put off the departure to Bradmore Road, something might change. This Mr. Burghclere might never arrive, for one thing. He sounded like a vague and elusive man, and anything might happen between here and Italy.

When Monday came, Mrs. Clomper took Maria to school herself. They walked silently up the broad, tree-lined expanse of St. Giles, past the trickle of young men who were emerging from St. John's College to go to early lectures. If only I were grown-up and school were all finished with, like it is for them, Maria thought miserably. I wonder if they know just how lucky they are. And full of envy she watched them pass, talking cheerfully to one another, calling and laughing, without a care in the world, it seemed.

Outside the railings that hemmed in the prim front garden of the Oxford Ladies' College there was a figure lurking. Streams of girls were passing through the gates all the time, but this one was waiting, in spite of the cold wind. As Maria and Mrs. Clomper drew near, the girl darted toward them. It was Harriet, very pink and eager.

"I thought I'd wait for you," she blurted out in an embarrassed way. "Just to show you where our cloak-rooms are, and where we go for prayers."

"Well, that's very nice of you, I'm sure," said Mrs.

Clomper. "I hope you haven't been waiting in this wind long, Miss Harriet."

"It's all right, I'm not cold," Harriet assured her. "But I wanted to be here in time so as not to miss you."

"Very nice, I'm sure," repeated Mrs. Clomper. "Well then, Miss Maria, I'll say good-bye. I'll be here at half past three, when you come out of school."

Harriet put out her hand eagerly, as though to take Maria's, and then, blushing deeply, thought better of it and thrust it behind her back. Chattering busily to cover up this mistake, she led the way around the side of the school buildings toward the cloakrooms.

"I expect you'll be in a much higher form than me. Papa says you know so many things. But it'll be all right if you put your hat and coat on the peg next to mine, and we can go into prayers together to begin with."

In the end Maria found herself in a set quite high up the school for Greek and Latin, working with girls several years older than herself. She was not very good at mathematics, but Uncle Hadden had taught her more than most girls learn, so that she was in a moderately high set for that. But as far as ordinary subjects went, like French and geography and botany, she was very far behind, and she was placed in a low form, Harriet's form. Harriet greeted her eagerly. At least, her face was eager even though it was not possible to say anything when the vice principal who had been questioning

Maria brought her to the Lower Fourth classroom.

"Here is a little girl for you, Miss Ferguson," the vice principal said. "She is quite good in some subjects, but she will have to stay in the Lower Fourth until she has caught up with the rest of the lessons."

With her head hung low, miserably embarrassed at having to walk in front of all those staring eyes, Maria slunk to the empty desk that was pointed out to her. And when she did at last manage to raise her eyes, she saw on the blackboard a diagram of the thing that had caused her greatest suffering at school before—a drawing of the earth designed to show why day was day and night was night. Then it swept over her again, the terrible despair that she had known at Semphill House. This was school. There were five more years of it, five more years of grappling with subjects in which she had not the smallest possible interest, barked at by angry teachers, stared at by curious girls.

But for the time being, at any rate, nobody barked at her. In fact, nobody took much notice of her at all, and lesson succeeded lesson with Maria hardly aware of them, until a bell clanged loudly and everybody tossed books into their desks, slammed down the lids, and made for the door. Harriet waited for her, smiling anxiously.

"It's lunchtime now, boiled-beef day. Do you mind boiled beef? I think it's better than boiled mutton, but some of the girls make an awful fuss. They say they ought to be allowed to bring sandwiches, as the food is so bad, but Miss Raby won't allow that, she says we can't work in the afternoon unless we have a proper hot meal. I don't think the food is so bad though, and I'm always terribly hungry."

She led the way to the lunchroom, a huge room filled with long tables and chattering girls, and smelling very strongly of cabbage. Maria found herself squeezed on a bench between Harriet and another girl, so that she could hardly use her elbows to cut up the boiled beef when it came.

"Are you going to Miss Raby's Greek class this afternoon?" Harriet asked Maria.

"Miss Raby's Greek?" The girl on Maria's other side paused with a piece of beef halfway to her mouth. "She's not! I think I'd die if I had to do that. Beatrice says Miss Raby's so sarcastic that she makes the girls cry sometimes. Even Mabel Smalley, and *she's* a monitor."

"Maria's very clever," said Harriet timidly.

"She'll need to be," said the other girl dryly, and applied herself to her beef.

But in fact Maria did not find Miss Raby's class so terrifying. The worst part was finding her way to the right room through the throngs of girls walking briskly and purposefully down the corridors. Panting and anxious, she had to ask the way several times, and then was so nervous that she forgot the instructions as soon as they were given. She managed to reach the room only a few seconds before Miss Raby herself swept in; in fact she was still squeezing through to the one vacant desk at the far side as the last muted whisper broke off abruptly and the girls rose to their feet in a silence that was broken only by the authoritative ring of Miss Raby's boots advancing toward them down the corridor.

Maria had made great strides with her Greek when she was taught by Uncle Hadden. She had given several hours a day to it, and she found that the class was reading the same book of Homer that she had done with him only a few weeks before, the part where Odysseus is in Polyphemus's cave. When her turn came she could stand up and translate the passage quite fluently although she had not prepared it specially. Miss Raby said very little, only, "I see you have been well taught, Maria. You were fortunate to have such a distinguished classical scholar for your uncle." Maria sat down in a glow of pleasure, and for the next half hour forgot all about her unhappiness and her troubles in the pleasure of wrestling again with Greek, and listening to Miss Raby explaining it—which she did in a way that was so clear and so interesting that Maria felt it might almost have been Uncle Hadden.

But when the bell clamored at the end of the day, Maria's unhappiness returned. She realized now, though she had been able to forget it before, that she was not among equals, she was with a set of girls considerably older than herself, who very pointedly turned their backs on her and clustered together, chattering with an easy assurance that she could never achieve. Miserably she edged around them. She would have liked to ask somebody what work they were supposed to prepare, and where to get the right books, but after hesitating by the door for a few minutes, and seeing nobody that she could possibly approach, she wandered off toward the cloakrooms. There it was no better. Everybody seemed to have a friend to talk to and something very particular to say. There was much giggling and little shrieks of laughter and whispering of confidences. Nobody spoke to her, but they stared, she felt, and then hastily turned the other way if she looked in their direction. Periodically the teacher on duty in the corridor outside called "Silence, girls," and everybody put their hands over their mouths and giggled; then a minute later the twittering would start again. Maria at last found her hat and coat and struggled into them. She was just going out the door when Harriet hurried up, pulling on her gloves, her hat all askew.

"I hope it wasn't too horrible," she said anxiously. "School, I mean. It must be dreadful starting in the middle of a term. Was Miss Raby very sarcastic? Fancy you being in her class!"

"It was all right, thank you." Maria could not think of anything else to say, and there was a heavy silence. Harriet was looking at her beseechingly. "I hope you'll let me know if there's anything I can do. I mean, if you want to know anything about the school or anything." She put her hand out as she had in the morning, as though to take Maria's, and then, as before, thought better of it and thrust the hand behind her. "And I do hope we'll be friends, and I am looking forward to you coming to live with us," she blurted out in a rush, and then ran away.

In the Library

*M*aria watched Harriet running down the path and out of the gate, and then, when she had disappeared, made her way toward the road. She could see the stout, erect figure of Mrs. Clomper waiting there.

"I'm glad you're not late, Miss Maria. I must say I could have done without coming to meet you today. There's a telegraph from Mr. Burghclere. It seems he's just gotten to England and he's traveling straight down to Oxford tonight. He'll be staying at the Eagle, I'm thankful to say, but still, I've got enough to think about without traipsing up here."

Maria stood still in the middle of the pavement. "Mr. Burghclere?" she said dully. This was the signal for her departure, for the end of the Lodgings, for the beginning of a new life in Bradmore Road. She had not expected it to be so sudden, she had thought there would be a few days' warning.

"I told you he would be arriving anytime," said Mrs. Clomper impatiently. "Now, come along, do, Miss Maria. There's so much I've got to do at home, and look, these young ladies want to get past."

Turning, Maria saw a group of the very same senior girls she had eyed in Miss Raby's class. They were looking at her, she felt sure, with amused disdain. She squeezed herself back against the wall to let them go past. Then she turned back to Mrs. Clomper.

"What time will Mr. Burghclere be coming?"

"That I can't say. It might be before dinner, it might be after. But his dinner's no concern of mine, he'll be eating out, I dare say."

When Mrs. Clomper rang the Lodgings bell, it was Lizzie, the little kitchen maid, who opened the door, and Maria remembered then that all the rest of the servants would have left today. The house as she stepped inside felt oddly still and deserted. It had always been a quiet house, of course, but somehow there had been a sense of people moving around it behind closed doors. Mrs. Clomper disappeared at once to attend to the hundred and one things that she said needed doing, and Maria wandered upstairs to her bedroom. Perhaps it was the last night that it would be hers, almost the last time that she would see it by daylight. And she stared around it, trying to fix it in her mind forever, letting her eye dwell on things that she had hardly bothered to take in before—the tall mahogany double-leafed wardrobe, the curved chest of drawers, the huge pier glass swinging on its frame, and above all, the view that she loved so much of the college quadrangle lying below her window. She crouched in the window until Lizzie came to tell her that dinner was ready, and after dinner she returned there, staring through the panes at the massive tower of the chapel opposite, at the patches of lighted window from undergraduates' rooms, at the quad itself, deserted except for an occasional hurrying figure striding over the flagstones in the chill wind.

Then it came over her that within a few hours Mr. Burghclere would arrive to take possession of all that was in the house. If she wanted to look at it for the last time, she must go at once; there would be no chance after tonight. So she crept out of her room, down the broad passage lined with dark oak doors, all tightly shut. These were bedrooms, never used, most of which she had never even been into. Occasionally through half-open doors she had seen them shrouded in dust sheets. Down the shallow oak stairs she went. She had never noticed that the banisters were carved like that,

that the grandfather clock in the hall below had a gold ball on top. She seemed to be seeing things for the first time as well as for the last. But the grandfather clock had stopped now; the man who came in to wind up the Lodgings clocks every Monday had not been there since Uncle Hadden died. Maria looked up at the polished brass face with real remorse. Letting a clock run down was like letting somebody starve to death. Perhaps it was the first time it had stopped since it was made — how could they have been so cruel! Then she tiptoed on down the hall, over the thick red and blue Turkey carpet. She peeped in at the drawing room. She did not have any feeling for this room; her uncle had rarely used it. It was full of stiffly arranged chairs of the upright sort, glass-fronted cupboards, and glass-topped tables with silver and gold trinkets on them, and there were no books and no really comfortable chairs.

The dining room was the next room. She had had breakfast there with Uncle Hadden every morning, sitting with him at the far end of the immensely long table, and making tea for both of them from the silver kettle over its little spirit lamp. She had seen the table when it had been laid for dinner parties, all the twenty-foot length of it sparkling with crystal, with silver candelabra and epergnes. And on Saturdays and Sundays she and her uncle had eaten their roast beef or roast mutton there, not saying very much, but looking contentedly over the Lodgings garden and the immaculate lawns, which had been there, her uncle told her, for three hundred years.

Farther down the hall lay the library. She hesitated before turning the handle. She had never in her life gone into the room without knocking first, and even now it seemed so much a part of Uncle Hadden that she could hardly bring herself to disturb it. More than this, the room had taken on a special character. Uncle Hadden had died there, his coffin had lain there. She hesitated, undecided. But the library was the room she loved best in the whole house; she would never be able to forgive herself if she left without seeing it one last time. She pushed the door open a crack and peeped in, as if afraid that the coffin might still be there, or the trestles that had supported it.

But there was nothing like that. The room felt rather damp and chill, as it had never felt in Uncle Hadden's time. It was distressingly neat, no papers strewn about, the desk bare, holding only the heavy silver-topped inkwell, the red leather blotter, the ivory paper knife.

But the smell of the old leather bindings was there, and all the books were still ranged around the walls as they always had been. Nobody had touched these yet. Still feeling like an intruder, Maria came inside and shut the door quietly behind her. On either side of the door were the shelves of theological works. Under the windows were the folio volumes, huge dictionaries and lexicons and atlases, and behind her uncle's desk, so that he could reach many of them without getting up, were the Greek and Latin authors that he valued more than anything else in his library. Maria remembered the loving way he had handled them and how he had talked about them to her. Much of it she had not been able to understand—what a waste it was, when he had been, as Miss Raby had said, one of the greatest scholars of his time.

She wandered past those shelves to the books she had enjoyed most, the editions of the English authors, Scott in red morocco, Shakespeare and other seventeenth-century plays that she had read, puzzled by much of them but enjoying herself all the same. There was a lot of poetry; curious old-fashioned novels printed a hundred years ago or more—she had read anything she fancied, nothing had been forbidden to her, and her uncle had seemed to take great pleasure in finding her sitting on the floor with a book spread open on her knees and books all round her. She ran her fingers now over the backs of some of the books. Smollet, Fielding, Richardson, Defoe, she had read most of those at one time or another.

The last one in the line was Defoe's *Journal of the Plague Year*. Idly she took it out and opened it, and then, because it was getting dark and she could not see well, she carried it over to the window. Before she realized what she was doing, she was deep in it, forgetting everything in the account of the deserted London streets, the mounting death rate, the crosses on the doors of the plague-stricken houses, the pits in which they tipped the dead.

She did not hear the doorbell, the voices in the hall. She read on through it all, murmuring to herself with irritation as the light got dimmer and dimmer, and kneeling on the chair near the window and holding the book to catch what light there was. She noticed nothing until there was the sound of a hand laid on the doorknob. Then she came to her senses, let the book fall into her lap, and sat bolt upright, her heart pounding. She felt almost suffocated with fright. On a sudden impulse she ran over to the far side of the room, to a dark corner that was screened by the massive globe of the world standing on the floor in its carved frame. Hardly knowing what she was doing, she crouched down behind. The door opened and somebody came in with a lamp.

"Just put it down on the desk," she heard a man's voice say. "I will light the gas myself."

Maria buried her face in her arms. Footsteps came over the carpet toward her, something was put down on the desk. "If there's anything else, Mr. Burghclere," she heard Mrs. Clomper's voice say. "Some Madeira and biscuits, perhaps? The poor warden always liked the decanter brought in at this time."

"No, no, thank you," said the man's voice rather impatiently. "I just want to glance through the shelves and then I must go back to the Eagle."

The library door closed, and a second or so later Maria heard a sigh of relief. That sigh helped to bring her to her senses. She felt like a spy; she had no business to be there listening to somebody sighing. The longer she stayed behind the globe, the worse it became. She stood up to see the tall figure of a man on the other side of the room holding a match to a gas bracket by the window. The room sprang into sudden brilliant light.

"I'm sorry," said Maria humbly. "I'm here."

The man jumped (Maria had jumped often enough herself, but she had never seen anybody else do it), and swung around. He was a tall, fair man with hair growing a little thin on his temples, though he looked quite young, and with a rather beaky, birdlike face.

"Why, upon my soul," he said, staring at Maria. "Who in the world are you? The housekeeper's little girl?"

"I'm Maria Henniker-Hadden. I lived here with Uncle Hadden."

Mr. Burghclere frowned a little and held his chin. He looked at Maria in an abstracted way. "Why, yes," he said at last. "There was a child, I remember Cousin

Henry writing to me to that effect. But I thought you would have been at school."

"I am going to school," said Maria.

Mr. Burghclere's face brightened. "That's all right, then. I thought for one moment that I was expected to take you over with the library." Maria said nothing; there did not seem to be anything that she could say. Perhaps Mr. Burghclere felt he had been a little unkind, for he said after a pause, "And how old are you—Maria, is it? And have you been living here long?"

"I'm twelve," Maria said. "I came to live at the Lodgings nearly two years ago, when Great-Aunt Lucia died."

"Do you like Oxford?" Mr. Burghclere was fingering the books by Uncle Hadden's desk as though he were longing to begin looking through them.

"I think it's the most beautiful place in the world," said Maria with feeling. "I'd like to live here forever and ever."

Mr. Burghclere seemed to be startled by the emotion with which she spoke. He stopped fingering the books and stared at her. "Would you now? I don't suppose you've seen Florence, then, or Rome, or Venice?"

"No," said Maria, remembering that the only other places she knew were Bath and that dull red-brick Midland town where she had been at boarding school.

"Oxford isn't such a bad place," conceded Mr.

Burghclere, "when the undergraduates are on vacation. Dreadful climate though. I suppose it's possible in September and the early summer. But Italy is the place, you know."

Maria was silent. Mr. Burghclere turned again to his books rather wistfully, and she realized she must go. "I'm sorry I disturbed you," she said, miserable. Then she looked at the book in her hand. "I was just looking at this. Could I put it back, please?" She went over to the shelf from which she had taken it.

"By all means. What is it you were reading? Defoe? I didn't know young ladies read Defoe. Dear, dear, what will your governesses say to that!"

Maria looked at him, frightened. She was not sure whether he was teasing her, or whether she had done something very improper. "I used to read everything when Uncle Hadden was here. I think he liked me to read. He didn't say there was anything I shouldn't look at."

"An excellent system, but not one that schoolmistresses and governesses will usually allow. I am afraid you are in for a hard time now, Maria."

Mr. Burghclere had an amused expression on his face, and Maria felt very confused. She struggled to defend herself. "It was not just Defoe that I read, I used to look at all the books. Except perhaps the theology. Though I did read Paley's *Evidences* and some of Jeremy

Taylor." She looked pleadingly at Mr. Burghclere, hoping he would say she had done nothing wrong.

"Are you fond of reading, then?"

"Oh, yes," said Maria fervently.

Mr. Burghclere seemed to consider. "Suppose you were to choose a book from the library. Would that be a memento of the days that you used to spend with Cousin Henry here?"

"It's very kind of you," said Maria.

Mr. Burghclere waved his hands at the walls. "You may make a choice, then. And if you'll forgive me, I'll attend to other things. My time here is so limited." He picked up a list from the desk which he scrutinized and then scanned the shelves. This made it easier for Maria. Nothing is worse than having to make a choice in a hurry with somebody watching you. She ran over to the shelves of English authors. But these were all in sets, and she did not know that she wanted any one of them so very particularly. It was the classical authors that she associated with Uncle Hadden, and she wandered over to the wall that was lined with them. The gaslight threw a brilliant white glow here, and she stooped and ran her eye over the titles. *Vergili Opera, Q. Horati Flacci Carmina*—she had read Virgil and Horace with Uncle Hadden, and she had rather liked Virgil.

"I should look somewhere else. You won't find much to amuse you there, I fancy." Maria gave a start and turned around; she was squatting on her heels and she peered up at Mr. Burghclere, who was towering above her with a benign smile.

"Would you rather I didn't take one of these?" she said nervously, wondering whether he thought they were too valuable to part with.

"Oh, you can have one of them with pleasure, but isn't it better to have something you can read? There's a nice little book with some engravings of Oxford over there, or a Buffon with some pretty animal pictures in it. Isn't that the sort of thing children like?"

Maria fingered the handsome binding of the Virgil. "I can read Virgil, though I have to prepare it in advance." The crouching position was becoming painful, so she straightened herself, and as she stood up her eyes rested on the shelf where Uncle Hadden kept his collection of little vellum-bound volumes printed by Aldus Manutius in Venice in the sixteenth century. "My Aldines" Uncle Hadden used to call them, and though he had told Maria that they were of no very great value, they were the books that he seemed to have the greatest affection for. When he read with her it was out of these copies, because he said that the print was so beautiful that it was a pleasure just to look at it.

"Could I have this, do you think?" Maria pulled out the *Odyssey.*

Mr. Burghclere came and stared over Maria's shoulder. "Now, why in the world do you want that?"

"We used to read it together, Uncle Hadden and I."
Maria was put out by Mr. Burghclere's tone of incredulous amazement.

"You read Greek?" Mr. Burghclere frowned at her.
"Read me some," he commanded.

Maria's lips were dry and her hands trembled as she
turned to the passage that she had been reading with
Miss Raby that very afternoon. In a shaky voice she
read first in Greek and then translated into English how
Odysseus and his men had lashed themselves under the
rams to escape from the giant Polyphemus's cave, and as
she got accustomed to the sound of her own voice she
forgot to feel frightened. It gave her such a delicious
sense of power to know exactly what the Greek meant
and to be able to supply just the right English word
without any hesitation. She came to the bottom of the
page and looked up with pleasure.

"It's lovely reading out of these Aldines. The print
looks so beautiful, it was that more than anything else
that made me want to hurry and learn Greek well
enough to read from them. Uncle Hadden said they
were made specially small so that people could carry
them in their pockets, and we could be sure that they
had been really read, not just stood on people's bookshelves. That's why I like them too." Then Maria
stopped, abashed. "But I expect you know all this, of
course."

But Mr. Burghclere handed her another book. "Try some of this." It was Horace's *Odes.* Maria could make sense of some lines, but she was not very fluent, and she was not pleased with herself.

"Now this." He put a third book into her hands.

"This is Italian," said Maria, frightened. "I don't know Italian. Uncle Hadden explained what letters had been changed when Latin turned into Italian, but I don't know anything else."

"Try it," said Mr. Burghclere, and he supplied words as Maria fumbled. She was interested, grappling with this language that looked so like Latin and yet was not, and lost all sense of time, so that she felt exasperated only when there was a knock at the door. It was infuriating to be interrupted.

"So you're *there,* Miss Maria," said Mrs. Clomper's outraged voice. "And here Lizzie and I have been up and down these stairs calling for you, looking for you. All over the place we've been. Come out this very minute. I'm sure I can't think what's come over the child," she said apologetically to Mr. Burghclere. "She's a quiet enough little thing as a rule and keeps herself to herself. Now come up to bed this instant, Miss Maria."

And Maria, red with confusion, her head hanging low, crept out of the room.

4

Maria's Departure

*M*aria appeared at breakfast the next morning deliberately late, hoping that by this ruse she would escape some of the scolding that Mrs. Clomper was sure to carry over from the night before. She also tried to draw a red herring over the trail.

"When shall I start packing up my things for Bradmore Road?" she asked in a voice that tried to be casual. "Shall I do some now, before I go to school?"

"You are not to go to school this morning," said Mrs. Clomper sternly.

Maria stared at her. Was this a punishment? Who had ordered it? "Is it because of last night?" she said in a small voice.

"I know no more about it than yourself, Miss Maria.

The last thing Mr. Burghclere said before he left was that he would like to see you in the morning, and when I said that you would be going to school, he asked very particularly that you should stay at home this morning, and that he would be coming in about ten o'clock. And as you know, I am not one for wasting time, Miss Maria, so I suggest that you spend the next two hours doing a little clearing up in your bedroom. Lizzie and I have quite enough to do without running around after you. I'll tell her to bring your boxes down."

Mrs. Clomper always made you feel you were in the wrong, Maria thought as she stood dolefully by the empty trunks in her bedroom. She had *offered* to do some packing, and then Mrs. Clomper had ordered her to do it in a tone that suggested Maria was forever shirking things. She wondered apprehensively what it was that Mr. Burghclere wanted to speak to her about. Surely he was not going to scold like Mrs. Clomper; he had seemed quite ready to talk to her last night; in fact, it was he who had kept her in the library when she had been perfectly willing to run away.

What with brooding over this and wandering aimlessly over to the window to look out on the quadrangle, she had done very little packing by the time she heard the doorbell ring in the distance. Footsteps went down the hall toward the library. She listened, hugging her little writing desk, which she had just brought in from the room she used as a sitting room. Footsteps came up the hall again and mounted the stairs. Maria hastily put the desk at the bottom of a trunk and looked around for something else to thrust in. One writing desk did not make much of a showing for an hour in her bedroom. But when Mrs. Clomper appeared at the door, she did not examine the trunks.

"Mr. Burghclere will see you now," she said grimly. "You will find him in the library."

Maria nervously smoothed down her dress and pushed back her hair as she hurried down. It was a shock to hear Mr. Burghclere's voice answering her tap on the door, even though she was expecting it. He was standing by the window in a heavy overcoat with an astrakhan collar.

"Good morning. I remembered Oxford as cold, but not as cold as this. It is my belief that this wind blows straight from Siberia, gathering up a little extra damp from the Thames valley on the way. And of all the uncivilized hostelries, the Eagle is the worst. Well, I can bear it no longer. I am going back to London, and you must follow me as soon as they can get you ready."

Maria did not understand. She thought he must mean that he wanted her out of the house as soon as possible, and she remembered guiltily how little progress she had made with her trunks. "I have started packing," she said anxiously. "I expect Mrs. Clomper will help me with my clothes."

Mr. Burghclere held his chin between his forefinger and his thumb. "The housekeeper. Yes, she might be the answer. What are her plans when she leaves Oxford, do you know?"

"She said she was going to stay with her sister in Banbury."

"Still, she might be open to persuasion. Banbury does not sound like the ultimate paradise for the Mrs. Clompers of this world. Do you and she agree fairly well?"

Again Maria was at a loss to know what he meant. As if a child could *disagree* with an adult! "I don't know," she said doubtfully. "We don't always like the same things, I suppose."

"But do you quarrel? Warring females under my roof I could not abide at any price. It would be impossible to work, think, derive any pleasure from life at all."

"Oh, no, we don't quarrel," said Maria, aghast at the very thought.

"Very well, we shall ask her, then. It would certainly save a great deal of trouble; it would be difficult to find a suitable female at such short notice. Besides, there would be the irritation of interviewing them, which I suppose I could not leave to you. I take it that you are agreeable?"

"To Mrs. Clomper, do you mean?" Maria was completely bewildered. "She is rather cross sometimes, but I don't think she really minds me. She did once say that I wasn't any bother."

"Agreeable to Mrs. Clomper is an advantage, certainly. But what I meant was agreeable to exchanging England for Italy?"

Maria had no notion at all what Mr. Burghclere could possibly mean. The conversation had been getting stranger and stranger, and she began to wonder whether she had left her senses, or whether perhaps Mr. Burghclere's had left him. "Do you mean you want to take Mrs. Clomper to Italy?" she said at last.

"I do not particularly want to take Mrs. Clomper to Italy, but if you are to come back with me, you will need a female companion of some sort."

"Me go to Italy?" Maria was stupefied.

"I think it would be of great benefit to you. You could then learn Italian properly. You have a distinct aptitude for the ancient languages, and what better place for pursuing them than in Italy? It will be interesting to see how you develop out there."

"You mean I will go to school there?" said Maria nervously.

"*School?* The Italians know better than to send their daughters to school. No, you can learn the classics with me, as you did with Cousin Henry. I will ground you in Italian, and the rest will be all around you—buildings, pictures, museums, and the very stones of Italy breathe culture! I have a good library at the Villa Gondi, and Cousin Henry's books will be coming out there—and what better education could you have than that?"

"I am going to Italy now?" repeated Maria, incredulous. "But where will I live?" She remembered Mrs. Clomper's remark that Mr. Burghclere did not have a home of his own, "not what you'd call an establishment."

"At the Villa Gondi, with me, where else? It's a fine house, up above Feronia, a small town which has the advantage of not being too far from Florence, yet far enough to prevent one being disturbed by acquaintances who are visiting Florence."

"And when am I going?" said Maria breathlessly.

"Just as soon as I get things settled here and arrange for the books and other objects to be moved to the Villa Gondi. Now, send me the good Mrs. Clomper, if you will."

Maria pounded up the stairs and flung herself into the housekeeper's room without even knocking. Mrs. Clomper had a pile of dusters which she was counting, and was completely taken by surprise when Maria threw her arms around her and buried her head on Mrs. Clomper's stout black shoulder. Maria was rather surprised at it herself, she so very rarely hugged or kissed anybody.

"Oh, Mrs. Clomper, we're to go to Italy. At least Mr. Burghclere's going to ask you to go too. You will, won't you? Oh, please do, he's waiting for you in the library now. And he *has* got a house of his own, it's near Florence, and it must be quite big because it's got a library, so I expect you'd be very comfortable."

"I really don't know what you're talking about, Miss Maria," said Mrs. Clomper, who had been nearly thrown off balance by Maria's sudden swoop upon her. "It's my belief that you've taken leave of your senses. What's all this about Mr. Burghclere wanting to see me?"

"In the library, now," said Maria urgently. "And you will say yes, won't you?"

"I'll say whatever I think it my duty to say," said Mrs. Clomper sternly, and she marched out of the room. But Maria was so elated that she seized Mrs. Clomper's pile of checked dusters and flung them up to the ceiling so that they scattered like confetti all over the room, and Maria was still rescuing one of them from behind a tall-boy in the corner (the only way to reach it was to lie flat on her front and reach with a long arm underneath) when Mrs. Clomper came back.

"Miss Maria, what in the world do you think you are doing? Get up this instant. Now, just look at your dress." Mrs. Clomper pointed grimly to the front of Maria's black dress. It had bits of fluff and carpet fibers sticking all down it; that was the worst of black alpaca, it always looked dusty. Maria gave it a perfunctory rub with her hand.

"Mrs. Clomper, are you coming? To Italy, I mean?"

"I told Mr. Burghclere that in the circumstances I thought it would be my duty to accompany you, Miss Maria. I do not suppose I shall care for foreign ways, but as I told Mr. Burghclere, I am sure it is what the poor warden would have wished."

Maria felt dampened. "But won't you *like* Italy at all?"

"I doubt it, Miss Maria. England is good enough for me any day. But when there is duty to be done, it is not my habit to shirk it. Now, how have you progressed with your trunks?"

There were other things to be done beside the packing, of course. Mr. Burghclere agreed, reluctantly, that he would have to see Mr. Josephs in London. Having to meet people, to talk to them, clearly was a great toil to him, but in this case there was nothing else to do. Maria was a ward in Chancery and she could not be taken to Italy without the lawyers' permission. But this interview with Mr. Josephs and a short letter to the Oxford Ladies' College was as far as he would go. Maria and Mrs. Clomper between them must settle with the Jessops, he said. They were not his concern at all, and in any case he was exhausted by the burden of arrangements that had fallen on him during this visit.

So a couple of days later Maria, accompanied by Lizzie, walked up to Bradmore Road to say good-bye to the Jessops. She had written a letter before this, but Mrs.

Clomper had insisted that this was not enough, that it was only polite to go and thank Mrs. Jessop for being so kind, and say she was sorry for having put her to any trouble. Maria knew that Mrs. Clomper was right, but she had hoped that perhaps she would be stopped from going because there was no time, or that Mrs. Clomper would say that the letter would do. But all Mrs. Clomper had said was that she could not possibly go with Maria, that she must take Lizzie, which made things even more difficult, because Lizzie could not prompt Maria or speak for her.

There was a chill dampness in the air as they walked up to north Oxford, and Maria thought how pleasant it was to be able to leave this behind, in only four days now. If things had worked out as they had originally been planned, she would have spent all her days walking up and down this ugly road, trying to think of things to say to Harriet Jessop. As it was, in a week's time she would be under blue skies in Italy, free of school and schoolgirls forever. And she gave a little skip of excitement.

Lizzie did not know this end of Oxford at all, and Maria had to lead the way to Bradmore Road, and even to ring the bell at the Jessops' house, for Lizzie was overcome by shyness and drew back nervously. The door was opened by a maid who recognized Maria.

"Is Mrs. Jessop at home?" Maria asked, fervently

hoping that Mrs. Jessop might be engaged on one of her committees.

"Oh, yes, miss. They're all in the sitting room at tea. I'll go and tell them that you're here."

This was the worst thing that could have happened, Maria thought as she waited in the cold hall, Lizzie shrinking behind her. There could be nothing more embarrassing than interrupting people in the middle of eating. The sitting room door opened and Mrs. Jessop came out.

"Why, Maria, how do you do? It is very nice of you to call. You will come in for a moment, will you not?"

Maria could not refuse, and, leaving Lizzie behind, she followed Mrs. Jessop into the sitting room. There they sat, Dr. Jessop and Harriet, beside a tea tray that had been placed in front of the fire. Maria averted her eyes, hoping and hoping that she would not be pressed into taking tea with them; hoping that she would not be thought to be expecting tea. Harriet and her father stood up, Harriet contriving to slop tea into her saucer as she did so, which made her blush and look uneasily at her mother.

"Well, Maria, it's sad that you won't be one of us after all," said Dr. Jessop, his thumbs in his waistcoat pockets. "We'd been looking forward to it, all of us. This house is a good deal too quiet and we'd like another daughter. Poor old Hetty is very cast down, eh, Hetty?"

"Oh, Papa!" Harriet shuffled uncomfortably with her feet.

"Yes, we would have enjoyed having you, Maria," said Mrs. Jessop very kindly for one who looked so austere. They all three of them stood, looking at Maria, who began to feel very uncomfortable.

"It was just that Mr. Burghclere decided," Maria began, not really knowing what she was trying to say. "He was Uncle Hadden's cousin, you know—well, a sort of second cousin, I think."

"Oh, yes, we quite understand," said Mrs. Jessop. "It is better that you should be with relations, after all."

There seemed no more to be said, so Maria shook hands all around, and said that she thought she ought to get back, that Mrs. Clomper was waiting for her. They all came with her to the door, and Harriet contrived to squeeze near her.

"Do you think you could possibly write?" she whispered. She was clenching and unclenching her hands in her nervousness. "Or perhaps I could write if I have your address?"

"I haven't been told what the proper address is. All I know is that Mr. Burghclere's house is called the Villa Gondi, and he said it was outside a town called Feronia, which is somewhere near Florence." She did not see how this information could possibly be enough for anybody who wanted to write a letter, but it appeared to satisfy Harriet, who nodded her head and seemed to be trying to memorize it.

"That's right," said Dr. Jessop, coming up behind them and putting his hand heartily on Maria's shoulder. "You write and let us know how you're getting on. And if you ever get tired of the blue skies of Italy, there's always Bradmore Road, you know."

They stood at the doorway, all three of them, in spite of the raw evening, and waved good-bye as Maria and Lizzie went down the road. As she turned to wave, Maria felt a pang. Really, they were very kind. She remembered Mrs. Jessop's remark about Mr. Burghclere being a suitable guardian because he was a relation, and she felt guilty. If only they knew, Mr. Burghclere was so remotely connected as hardly to be a relation at all.

And as she walked back into Oxford again, she felt twinges of remorse. She looked around her as they drew near St. Giles; at the broad sweep of tree-lined road ahead of them, at the sober dignity of the judge's house with its high railings outside, the pleasant little church on the corner, the long frontage of St. John's College lying on their left. She sighed. Oxford was beautiful; perhaps in the end she would be homesick for it.

A Channel Crossing

The same pangs came over Maria as she looked out for the last time over Oxford from the windows of their railway carriage two days later. There were the towers and spires spread out before her, the spire of the University Church, the dome of the Radcliffe Camera, the Cathedral, Tom Tower. Surely even Italy could not be as beautiful as this? But then a gust of wind blew rain across the windows, and she thought of herself trudging down the Banbury road day after day through weather like this to spend the day with hateful girls, and she rejoiced.

Whether Mrs. Clomper rejoiced was another matter. Maria looked at her anxiously from time to time throughout the journey to London. She had seemed particularly grim and aloof during the past week, and had answered Maria's eager questioning, "You *do* want to go to Italy, don't you, Mrs. Clomper?" with, "My duty is my duty, Miss Maria." Maria hoped that this was because everything was such a rush, that Mrs. Clomper would recover once all her responsibilities had been left behind. But now she glanced uneasily at Mrs. Clomper's forbidding face and wondered if she was angry because Mr. Burghclere had hurried her away from Oxford, at his insistence that furniture movers should deal with the crating of the books from the warden's library and the packing of all the furniture and objects that were to go to the Villa Gondi.

"You will see all Uncle Hadden's things again in Italy," said Maria timidly. "And Mr. Burghclere's house sounds very comfortable, just as comfortable as an English house."

Mrs. Clomper settled herself in an even more upright position. "We must wait and see about that, Miss Maria. Something called the Villa Gondi is not *my* idea of an establishment fit for English folk, and as for the poor warden's books, I shall be surprised if those Italians get *us* to Italy, let alone books and furniture."

In fact, they were not going straight to the Villa Gondi. Mr. Burghclere planned first to spend a week or two in Venice. He had been lent a house there, and he wanted to work on some manuscripts that could be seen only in Venice. Besides, he said, he wanted to show Maria the mosaics in St. Mark's, and to introduce her to the paintings of Bellini and Tintoretto. They were to spend two nights in London in a quiet hotel near Piccadilly, and near Albany, where Mr. Burghclere had an apartment. They could not leave any earlier, because Maria still had to have her interview with Mr. Josephs. The prospect of this interview was the only thing that clouded her happiness. Perhaps after all the cup was going to be dashed from her lips. The humiliation of being sent back to Bradmore Road, to the Oxford Ladies' College, at Mr. Josephs's orders, after all her triumphant farewells! "Please let him say yes, please let him say yes," she prayed next day as she and Mrs. Clomper waited in the little inner room underneath Mr. Josephs's office in the Temple.

But Mr. Josephs did not forbid her to go. He just looked at her keenly under his gray eyebrows. "Do you really want to go to Italy?"

"Oh, yes," said Maria fervently. "Please, I do very much."

"There is really no reason why you should not," said Mr. Josephs slowly. "Mr. Burghclere has undertaken to care for your education, and you will have Mrs. Clomper to accompany you. But it seems a solitary sort of life for a little girl. I should have thought you had been too long already without the company of young people. Dr. Jessop's plan, the original plan to bring you up with his own daughter, seemed such an excellent arrangement."

"But I'm used to being alone." Maria felt stiff with anxiety. "I prefer being by myself to being with other girls."

"That is a very great pity. It is never a good thing to cut oneself off from one's fellows. However, we will say no more. I have asked Mr. Burghclere to let me know of your progress, and he is to bring you here in six months' time, so that we can talk things over again, if necessary."

Maria emerged into the brisk March wind outside with a feeling that she had shed an enormous load. She was free now, everything was in order, and only Italy lay ahead. Two days later they traveled down to Dover, all of them in a first-class railway carriage. Mr. Burghclere had a mound of journals and expensive-looking art magazines beside him and never looked up from them. Mrs. Clomper apparently did not think it proper this time to go to sleep as she usually did in trains, and Maria, too excited to read (and in any case a little worried about what sort of book Mr. Burghclere would expect her to read) just stared out at the Kent countryside rushing past them. Spring was advancing a little now: There was a pale greenness in the hedges, the grass in the fields was brighter, there were lambs running about on stiff legs.

At Dover, the bustle, the formalities, the waiting,

the searching for porters, the counting of the luggage, all of which made Mr. Burghclere sigh wearily, only delighted Maria, and she thought that if it was so exciting before they even reached Italy, then Italy itself must be a paradise beyond her imagination. At last they were aboard the steamer, and Mrs. Clomper had counted every item of luggage three times, since she did not believe Mr. Burghclere's Italian valet, Giuseppe, to be either capable or honest. Mr. Burghclere had disappeared, and Maria knelt on the wooden bench at the side of the steamer, watching all the people coming up the gangway, and looking out over the turmoil on the quay.

Mrs. Clomper shook her shoulder. "Come along, Miss Maria. I have spoken to a sailor, and he says there is a ladies' saloon downstairs."

Maria turned a woebegone face to her. "Oh, but Mrs. Clomper, can't I stay? There's so much to see and I've never been on a ship before."

"Certainly not, Miss Maria. This is no place for a young lady. Besides, you will catch your death of cold, and then what'll I do with you, I'd like to know? Trying to nurse you in foreign parts! No thank you, you come downstairs this minute."

"Just until the boat goes, then," begged Maria.

Mrs. Clomper relented. Perhaps she thought she could keep a watchful eye on the luggage, stacked on the deck, and see that a mischief-making sailor did not take it into his head to hurl it off the ship. At any rate, she sat down on the bench beside Maria, though she did not watch the scene below on the quayside with Maria's eagerness.

It was such fun staring at people, Maria had never had such a chance before. There were not many children there, so she was fascinated to see advancing toward the gangway a procession of four girls, the oldest perhaps sixteen, the youngest eight or so, all dressed the same in dark green coats and little round hats with a green feather. They had long hair combed down their backs, three of them fair hair, and the fourth, a girl of about Maria's age, bright red hair. They were accompanied by a rather agitated elderly lady who could only be a governess, by two maids, and by several porters carrying quantities of luggage. With the air of much-experienced travelers they advanced up the gangway and Maria watched them eagerly. They really looked quite interesting, rather important sort of children, and she wondered who they were. But they did not stay on deck, and Maria turned her attention again to the quay and the other passengers.

The ship must be going to leave any moment now, she thought, as the siren was blowing noisily above their heads, sailors were unwinding the ropes and chains that bound the ship to the quay, the gangway had been lifted, and the deck quivered with the movement of engines. Then at last the ship begin to move. Her bow thrust away from the quay, and peering over the rails Maria could see white foam breaking on either side. The quayside retreated farther and farther from them, they were out in the middle of the harbor now, there was a wonderful smell of sea, and the sea gulls wheeled and shrieked overhead.

"Now, Miss Maria," said Mrs. Clomper with great firmness. Sighing, Maria got up and went with her to find the ladies' saloon. It seemed closed in and stuffy and overpoweringly full of ladies. Of course all the best seats had been filled by now and it was no longer possible to sit by the windows. How horrible it was down here, Maria thought, and supposing somebody was sick! All books of travels talked about seasickness, and she examined the faces of all the ladies to see if there was anybody who seemed to be in danger of it. She did not have to look far. Ranged underneath the windows, on a long seat upholstered in red plush, sat the four girls and their governess, and the governess was already suffering. She sat up with her eyes closed and a look of great misery on her face, while the eldest girl, who seemed very poised and efficient and sensible, held a bottle near her nose, and dabbed at her forehead with a handkerchief. The two youngest girls just stared at the poor governess with enormous curiosity, while the redhead sat with hands folded in her lap as though the affair were a commonplace one.

"How can poor Miss Buldino be ill if the ship hasn't hardly started?" inquired one of the younger girls in a penetrating voice.

"Hush, Sophy," the eldest girl rebuked her.

"It's probably the smell of the engines. Or of the food they're cooking," said the redheaded girl. "Anyway she *is* ill every time, so it is really pointless to ask."

At the mention of food, poor Miss Buldino groaned so that Maria could hear her. How stupid grown-ups were, she thought. They would be perfectly all right outside on the deck, but here, herded altogether, in this stuffy, smelly place, anybody would be made sick. And she began to notice how very disgusting the smell was, like rancid fat. In fact, the thought of the food they might be cooking in it made her feel almost ill herself. The trouble was, she could not stop thinking about it or stop smelling the smell, which seemed at last to be right inside her, as though she had eaten it and it had sadly disagreed with her. She stopped taking an interest in Miss Buldino, because the sight of the latter's drawn suffering face made her feel even worse.

She shut her eyes and wondered how much longer this journey was going on, and wished she knew whether her misery would be over in half an hour, an hour, five hours, or what. Only if it was to be five hours, then she supposed it was better not to know. Then she heard a voice nearby saying: "Perhaps the little girl would like some eau de cologne. We find it helps our governess."

Maria opened her eyes. She was not even embarrassed; she did not care in the least how many people knew how ill she was feeling. There stood the oldest of the four girls, holding out a bottle to Mrs. Clomper.

"Thank you, miss, I'm sure. No, Miss Maria doesn't look too well. We'll see what eau de cologne will do."

"Perhaps if you put it on a handkerchief and tied it around her forehead?" The girl hovered helpfully, with an air of somebody who was used to taking charge of things. "It is rather close in here, though it's a smooth crossing for this time of year."

The eau de cologne felt deliciously cold on Maria's head, and the smell revived her a little; she was able to take in her surroundings again. The girls in green coats had transferred their interest to her now. There they sat, the two little ones staring with shameless curiosity, the redhead giving her an occasional amused glance. Miss Buldino seemed to be asleep, her head was leaning back against the cushions, her mouth was a little open.

"Would you like a smelling bottle?" the eldest girl asked Maria in a sympathetic voice.

"Tell her that we shall be at Calais in fifteen minutes, Helena," called the redhead. "Don't you remember

Uncle Harry's joke? It isn't brandy that's the best cure for seasickness, it's port."

"Hush, Cordelia," said her sister reprovingly. "But it's true, we have not so very much longer to wait. Perhaps I ought to see what has happened to the maids. Let me know if there is anything else I can do for you."

Maria left everything to Mrs. Clomper; she just sat in a miserable huddle, listening to the excited chattering of the little sisters without really taking in that it must be the French cliffs that they were pointing out to each other. Eventually Mrs. Clomper helped her to her feet, and she stumbled out behind her, through the surge of ladies who were thronging the doors. The cold wind on deck seemed to hit her, and she shivered. It was like a cold bucket of water being thrown over her, but it helped bring her to her senses, and she remembered that she still had the smelling bottle in her hand. She looked around. The redheaded Cordelia was only a few feet away, standing by the rails of the ship in a cool, self-possessed way, as though she had done the journey so many times that it had become tedious. Maria thrust the bottle at her.

"Thank you," said the girl. "I'll give it back to Helena. You look rather unwell, I must say. Have you far to go?"

"Venice," said Maria faintly, feeling she did not want to travel another mile.

"There's another couple of days ahead of you, then. Still, it will be over land now." And with her sisters she moved down the gangway.

Maria and Mrs. Clomper stood waiting there for Mr. Burghclere and Giuseppe. Maria shivered in the keen wind and looked down at the quay. It seemed much the same as Dover, the same dingy collection of buildings behind, and a railway beyond that, the same bustle, except that here the porters wore blue smocks and seemed to shout rather louder. Maria noticed a magnificent personage in livery and heavy whiskers standing like a statue on the quay while the hurly-burly surged around him. She wondered with no very great interest who he might be; a servant of somebody important, a railway official perhaps. Then he advanced in a dignified way through the crowd, and Maria heard a voice that she remembered, saying, "Here's Mr. Mant, Miss Buldino."

There they were, the cluster of sisters in their green coats, the two maids, the governess, the mounds of luggage carried by porters. The tall, whiskered personage seemed to clear a way for them through the crowds, and Maria watched them disappear.

"Lord Rivingham's daughters," remarked Mr. Burghclere's voice at Maria's shoulder. "I did not know they were on this boat."

Maria was surprised. "Do you know them, then?"

"We are neighbors at Feronia," said Mr. Burghclere with such lack of interest that Maria did not care to ask any more questions.

After that there was a three-hour trip by train, during which Maria dozed most of the time, opening her eyes occasionally to see country that seemed exactly the same as the country they had passed through on the way to Dover. At Paris she was led in a daze to a cab which rattled through streets she was too tired to look at. Nor did she take much notice of the hotel when they reached it. She just sat on the edge of the huge bed while Mrs. Clomper bustled around with a grim face; she drank a cup of strange-tasting tea which a chambermaid brought in, stiffly and wearily undressed herself, and fell into the depths of a very deep feather mattress.

But next morning it was different. She woke to see sun creeping through cracks in the shutters, and stared puzzled at the brightly polished brass knobs on the foot of her bed, wondering what had happened to the mahogany rails she usually saw there. Then she remembered, and flung herself out of bed to peer through the chinks of the shutters to try to see what Paris really did look like. She was still there when Mrs. Clomper came in a few moments later, and she guiltily ran back to her bed.

"I wanted to see what France was like. I was too tired to notice yesterday."

"Tired!" said Mrs. Clomper. "I've never seen anybody in the state you were in last night, Miss Maria. I
almost had to undress you like a baby. And you'd left
London only a few hours before. It's a fine thing, I must
say, when you've months, not to say years, of living in
foreign parts ahead of you!"

"It wasn't foreign parts that made me tired," objected
Maria. "It was that dreadful smell on the ship."

"I can't say I noticed anything except the luncheon
cooking. Nor did those other young ladies either. And I
couldn't even get a nice cup of proper tea to give you.
They *called* it tea, but it wasn't. And they say they can
give us only coffee for breakfast. My word, but we've got
a bad time ahead of us. Not even curtains either!" Mrs.
Clomper flung back the shutters noisily.

"It's sunny, anyway," said Maria, trying to introduce
a more soothing subject. "Look how blue the sky is."

"A day that begins as bright as this always has rain by
the afternoon. Now, hurry up and get dressed, Miss
Maria, or they'll be bringing your breakfast."

Whatever Mrs. Clomper had to say about foreign
ways, Maria thought the breakfast was delicious. There
was an enormous bowl of very milky coffee, and some
delicious crescent-shaped rolls with a curl of pale butter. Not long after that they drove through Paris in
another cab. Maria was alert and excited now, and
looked out eagerly at the tall gray houses with their

shutters folded back against the walls, the wide streets, the river with its tree-lined walks on either side, the distant view of the cathedral of Notre Dame, which Mr. Burghclere pointed out, rather as an afterthought, as though he had forgotten Maria had never seen Paris before.

But the cab journey did not take very long and the train journey did. It stretched over a span of three meals and one night. It had never struck Maria before that a train journey could take so long, though when she considered it, she supposed that it could take far longer, if you wanted to go down to Naples, for instance, or to Moscow. But they were going only as far as Milan, and changing there into the train for Venice. They ate luncheon out of a hamper, dinner in the restaurant car, and then Maria and Mrs. Clomper retired into a sleeping compartment which they shared with two other ladies. Maria did not sleep particularly well, she always seemed to feel the wheels turning and turning below her and rushing through the night. She did not dare ask Mrs. Clomper the next morning how she had slept. She looked timidly at the good lady's martyred expression, and then wondered whatever she would say to another breakfast without tea, because if the French hotel could not produce it, then it was fairly certain that a train would not either.

But the worst part of the journey was really the last,

when they were within a few hours only of Venice. There were blue Italian skies, certainly, but under them stretched a dreary expanse of flat, flat land, unbroken as far as she could see. "The Lombardy plain," said Mr. Burghclere, and buried himself in a book. The Lombardy plain went on and on, and was flatter than anything Maria had ever seen. It was broken occasionally by a line of poplar trees, by a white road, by ditches, and that was all. Then gradually, imperceptibly, it changed, the ground became more uneven, they skirted a lake, high hills appeared in the distance, some of them even with snow on top. They stopped at stations with lovely names—Verona, Vicenza. Then the hills disappeared again, and the ground became flatter and more low-lying than ever. The long shadows of late afternoon turned to twilight, and then to dark. Maria had heard nothing about spending a second night on the train, but she did not dare ask Mr. Burghclere about the time of their arrival, for he seemed morose and silent. Then suddenly he looked out the window at the station they were rushing through. "Here's Mestre. We'll be in Venice in a few minutes." And he began piling his books and papers together.

Maria, kneeling at the window, alert and excited, saw that the railway line was over water now, and that there were pricks of light ahead of them which must mean Venice. A few minutes more and they were there, climbing stiffly down onto the ridiculously low platform, walking down through the crowd to the world outside. It was only when she emerged from the station that she really grasped how different Venice was from anywhere else in the world. Where else would you walk down the steps of a railway station to find water instead of a street, dark, black water, with the light from the pale moon reflected in it?

Water and Mosaics

*I*f Mrs. Clomper had disliked the foreignness of everything that had happened to her in the last two days, then she must be near breaking point now, Maria reflected as she tucked her coat around her to make room for the two grown-ups on the low cushioned seat of what she supposed must be a gondola.

Outside the tiny tentlike cabin in which they sat, Giuseppe was supervising the loading of their luggage while a ragged-looking man was holding the prow of the gondola steady from the pavement. Then Giuseppe flung a coin onto the path above and the gondola moved off, out into the middle of the canal. The ragged man shouted angrily and Giuseppe shouted back, and the exchange of abuse went on, like two dogs seeing who could bark last. Then the distance defeated them both and there was sudden silence in which all that could be heard was the lap of water against the side of the boat, and the splash as their boatman, standing up behind them, moved his oar.

The sky was very clear and starry, the water like black glass, and through the little windows on either side Maria could see huge pallid buildings with lighted windows here and there that were reflected on the water. The boat seemed so frail and small to be carrying all of them and their luggage in the middle of this huge expanse of water, and Maria began to fret and wonder how deep it was, and what lay at the bottom. And if she felt this, she knew Mrs. Clomper must be thinking exactly the same. The boatman gave a hoarse, lugubrious cry, and the boat turned from the broad sweep of water into a narrower lane, if you could call something so watery a lane. Here it was much darker, and they moved between high, dark buildings against whose walls the water lapped with a hollow sound.

"Are they really built *in* the water?" Maria asked incredulously at last, the first question she had dared ask.

"They are built on wooden piles in the water, yes. How they continue to stand, one cannot say, but they do. One of the great beauties of Venice is her decay."

"So that's what you can smell all the time," said Mrs.

Clomper stiffly. "Decay and dry rot, I shouldn't wonder. All I can hope is that they have heard of such things as airing the sheets."

"Airing the sheets is a wholly English fad, I imagine," remarked Mr. Burghclere.

It now suddenly came upon Maria, sitting between the two of them, how very much Mr. Burghclere and Mrs. Clomper disliked each other. There was something exciting about it, like watching a dogfight, except that at a dogfight she could be a disinterested spectator, whereas in this fight she would suffer all the time from their irritation.

The boatman had stopped rowing, and the gondola drifted toward some steps rising out of the water. Then he jumped out and pulled the boat in. Mr. Burghclere rose to his feet, making the gondola dip and sway terrifyingly, and Maria, peering out of the window, could see nothing to get out for. At the top of the steps was a black nail-studded door that looked as if it had never been opened. Above it hung a feeble lantern, which showed a range of heavily grilled windows on either side. It looked as if they had arrived at a prison. Giuseppe helped her out on the slippery step, and then held out his arm to Mrs. Clomper. Mrs. Clomper pushed it angrily away and tried to get out unaided, but her step was uncertain and she would have fallen if Giuseppe had not seized her.

"The luggage, the luggage!" said Mrs. Clomper shrilly. "Don't let them go away with it. We'll never see it again."

"The luggage is in no danger," said Mr. Burghclere coldly, "but it seems that you are, unless you take Giuseppe's arm. I would not care to fall into the water fully clothed myself."

There was no time for further words, for at this moment the prisonlike doors were opened. Inside it was brightly lit, there were handsome marble floors, much gilded furniture, and palms and ferns in pots. It must be a hotel, thought Maria, blinking at the lights, and watching blue-overalled men swooping down on the luggage and tucking suitcases and bags under their arms. Then she was led away by Mrs. Clomper and a withered, elderly maid, up broad staircases and down long corridors, to a large, marble-floored bedroom, where she was made to go to bed.

Her first thought when waking the next morning was that this was not so very foreign. Nobody would guess that this room belonged to a house that had its feet and its cellars in the water. Admittedly, there were no curtains, and the floor was polished stone with no covering except mats by the bed and the washstand, but otherwise it was comfortable.

She said as much to Mrs. Clomper, who did not seem in the least impressed. "Stone floors are not *my* idea of comfort. Poverty-struck, I'd say. And you remember, Miss Maria, that we're seeing the best they can do. This is a hotel that has English visitors, and they have to mind their p's and q's for people who know what's what. But just you wait till Mr. Burghclere gets into that house that's been lent to him and we have Italian servants running around us and that wicked-looking Jooseppy! Then you'll wish you were back in the Lodgings!"

"Do you think we'll be able to see water from Mr. Burghclere's house?" Maria asked eagerly.

"See water!" said Mrs. Clomper sourly. "There's nowhere in the whole of this place where you can't see water. Another week and you'll be wishing it was a desert." She flung open the shutters and Maria ran over eagerly. At first she could see no water, just balconies and windows in the house opposite, which seemed extraordinarily near. Then, by standing on tiptoe and looking down, she could see the canal.

"Oh, look, there's a boat with furniture piled on top. Just think, Mrs. Clomper, even if you move house you have to go by boat!"

Mrs. Clomper shuddered. Perhaps she thought of the warden's books and furniture being transported across Italy in this way. "Only foreigners would have such nasty ideas. Now, come along, Miss Maria, and see if they can find breakfast for us."

More than anything, Maria was longing to see just how many canals there were, how you walked around Venice, how the houses could possibly be built on the water. But she did not get very far that morning. Mr. Burghclere left the hotel soon after breakfast, telling them that he had to arrange for them to move into the Palazzo Malipiero. Mrs. Clomper would perhaps take Maria for a little walk in the meantime.

"It is almost inevitable that you will lose your way. One always does in Venice," he said coolly as he stood in the hall of the hotel with Giuseppe handing him his gloves and his cane. "But you have only to say the name of this hotel, and anybody will conduct you back. Tonight, Maria, I will take you to see the mosaics in St. Mark's."

Mrs. Clomper was very indignant. "Ask an Italian the way!" she said furiously after Mr. Burghclere had gone. "I'd rather throw myself into all that dirty water. No, Miss Maria, we stay here. It's not my idea of spending a morning, but at least it's safe, I suppose."

But half an hour later she was not so sure. They were sitting in the hall, near a door which opened on to a sunlit path; Maria caught glimpses of it when people went in or out. She was staring at the door, aching to go through it herself, when Mrs. Clomper gave a sharp exclamation.

"Do you see that man?"

Maria looked around. "Which man?"

"Miss Maria, *please!*" hissed Mrs. Clomper. "Come, we had better go upstairs."

While they climbed the stairs, Mrs. Clomper told Maria, in a voice that trembled with agitation, of a man "of the lower orders, I would have said, but you never can tell with Italians," who had been staring and grinning in the most insolent way. But when they reached Maria's bedroom they found the door wide open and a dark-haired young maid sweeping the floor.

"Shall we go out, then?" said Maria. "We could always keep in sight of the hotel."

To her surprise, Mrs. Clomper agreed. She seemed to have been badly shaken by the grinning Italian, whoever he might have been, and hurried Maria through the hall faster than Maria had ever known her to walk before. The doorway gave on to a pavement with houses on the other side, and it was beautifully sunny outside. Maria looked around her carefully. She felt it was she rather than Mrs. Clomper who was in charge now, and she knew that she would have to conduct the walk. In one direction the pavement seemed to end in a canal. In the other direction there did not appear to be any water; the path wound on between houses. Maria pointed.

"If we walk slowly this way we can always turn back. The hotel is easy to find. Look, Hotel Grimaldi, we can't miss that," and she pointed to the large painted sign.

In fact, the path soon did come to water. They went around a corner and over a hump-backed bridge, and there was a canal, narrow and dark. Maria paused on top of the bridge and peered down.

"Come away at once, Miss Maria, or you'll fall in. And now that I come to think of it, we'd better turn back and make sure the hotel's still there. I wouldn't trust anything in this land."

So they went back and the hotel was still there. But so was the Italian of "the lower orders." He was standing at the door this time, leaning on a long broom, and at the sight of him Mrs. Clomper turned around at once and marched Maria back the way they had come. They turned the corner, crossed the hump-backed bridge, and went on down the path, which seemed to become narrower and darker, and the houses on either side taller, blotting out more of the sky.

Then suddenly they emerged in a sunny square with an impressively grand church on the other side. The warm spring sun struck up at them from the stones of the pavement, and from the buildings that surrounded the square; pigeons cooed in a continuous low rippling, and the air was full of the sounds of people chattering, children calling, footsteps. It took Maria a moment or two to realize what was strange about the sounds. Then

she knew. They were town sounds without the usual
noise of traffic to drown the voices and the footsteps.
She had never been so conscious of footsteps before.
She would have liked to have stayed there, just listening, and watching the young women who were drawing
water from a well in the middle of the square, and chattering and laughing. But then they hung their filled
buckets one on each end of a bow-shaped piece of wood
which rested across a shoulder and walked off with
them, and the square was left to the children.

Mrs. Clomper would allow no more lingering. She
marched Maria briskly around the square. "I'm keeping
my eye on that lane we came out of, Miss Maria. Once
you take your eye off that, you can give yourself up for
lost."

Then they plunged into the dark entry out of which
they had just come and hurried back to the hotel again.
But the "insolent" Italian who, to Maria's eye, just
looked friendly, was still there, smiling as much as ever,
and again Mrs. Clomper wheeled around and returned
to the sunny square.

"I'll do it all day if need be," she told Maria angrily.
"He's not going to think he's getting the better of me."

Six times they did that trip, with Mrs. Clomper
growing grimmer every trip. And they would have done
it a seventh time had they not met Mr. Burghclere, who
came around the corner just as they were about to

wheel around and march back again.

"That dreadful man," gasped Mrs. Clomper. "His impertinence! You must tell the manager of the hotel at once!"

"Which dreadful man?" Mr. Burghclere glanced around. "I can see only one of the hotel porters."

"That's him!" Mrs. Clomper, forgetting all correctness, pointed with her umbrella at the blue-overalled man who was now bowing and smiling in their direction.

"The porter. Mrs. Clomper, you astonish me. A more friendly being never stepped this earth. We have already hurt his feelings enough. We had better go inside."

Mrs. Clomper's feelings also seemed to be hurt, for she never said another word that day. Her face and her manner were stony and aloof. She spent the afternoon in her bedroom, which meant that Maria had to stay in hers too, staring down at the patch of canal visible from her window, or at the balcony of the house opposite. Mr. Burghclere had business to attend to, but he promised to come back to take Maria to see St. Mark's. She had not much idea of what St. Mark's was, except that it must be a church. But on the way there she would surely be able to see what Venice really looked like.

She had forgotten, however, what difference a silent and disapproving presence could make to enjoyment.

Mrs. Clomper was with them, grim, black, stony. Mr. Burghclere seemed able to forget about her, but Maria could not. She sat stiffly in the gondola, never once turning her head to see the places that Mr. Burghclere pointed out. The gondolier took them down the narrow canal where the hotel stood, out on to the broad, sunlit sweep of what Mr. Burghclere told Maria was "The Grand Canal—the *Canale Grande*, that winds like an S through Venice." Then he named all the buildings that they passed, pointing first to this side, then to that, until Maria was giddy with looking and dazed with the flow of Italian names. They all seemed to be palaces, and she was troubled by their lack of grandeur. All without exception had a neglected look, with falling stucco, crumbling brickwork, and stained stone.

"Is the palace where we are going to stay somewhere here?" she asked timidly.

"The Palazzo Malipiero is not on the Grand Canal, mercifully. There is to my mind something a little vulgar about staying on the Grand Canal. But you will learn these things."

Maria did not venture to make any other remark, but she wondered a little. If these grand houses were crumbling, then the Palazzo Malipiero must be even more decayed. The boat moved in to some steps, and a swarm of ragged youths sprung at it, jostling and quarreling as to who should hold it steady. Maria looked uneasily at Mrs. Clomper, who was drawing her skirts around her as though a pack of dirty mongrel dogs were approaching too near.

"*Gransiere*," remarked Mr. Burghclere coolly. "Which means crab catchers, only these wish to catch our money. You will have to accustom yourself to them, Mrs. Clomper, as well as to many other Venetian notions."

At this Mrs. Clomper uttered her only word of the afternoon. "*Never!*" she said in a voice that trembled with anger, and looking with furious disgust at the *gransiere*, she stepped onto the quay.

Mr. Burghclere guided Maria through the idling crowds that thronged the waterside; elegant, foppish young men twirling canes; black-haired, white-skinned ladies; and any number of ragged children and men who seemed to have nothing to do but loaf in the sun. "Spring and the sun brings them all out," he said, glancing around him. "Venice is a city of idlers, as you will soon discover."

Maria would very much have liked to loaf and idle herself, and stare over the sunlit water of the Grand Canal. She had been hurried all morning, and it was evidently to be the same now. They were the only people walking quickly; everybody else seemed to have unlimited time. They turned away from the water, up a pathway between tall buildings. Here were shops and cafés, people sitting at little sidewalk tables, and the air was full of chattering voices, music, guitars and violins, tinkling cups. Maria could have enjoyed it so much if she had been allowed to linger and look, and if she had not been so uncomfortably aware of the somber, disapproving presence of Mrs. Clomper. They turned a corner, went under an arch, and then stood in the most enormous square Maria had ever seen. Mr. Burghclere waved at it airily.

"The Piazza San Marco, the heart of Venice. And straight in front of you, St. Mark's."

"But it's so small!" Maria stared at the bizarre building in the distance. She had never seen a church like it. There were a mass of golden domes glinting in the bright sun. There seemed to be no windows but a line of blind arches filled with color—blue, pink, and gold. Altogether rather frivolous and gaudy, she thought, and not the least what a church should be like.

This remark seemed to please Mr. Burghclere. "It is small as cathedrals go. It was the chapel of the doges— the rulers of Venice."

"Yes, Oxford Cathedral is small because it's a college chapel," remarked Maria.

Mr. Burghclere gave her an approving look. "Precisely. I am glad I have made my point."

It seemed to take an immense time to cross the square. It was thronged with people who were ambling idly, greeting one another and chattering. There were soldiers in quaint uniforms like fancy dress, nurses with babies on their arm (each baby's face carefully veiled against the sun), young Venetian girls wearing black shawls walking about in twos and threes, ragged urchins scrambling and fighting for cigar ends. And pigeons everywhere, strutting over the stones so that all the time it seemed as though you would have to tread on them, only at the last moment they would sidle out of the way. The piazza was full of music, bands playing outside the cafés all around the edge of the square, and there was a murmuring of voices too, and the occasional loud clapping of wings as a flock of pigeons, startled by some noise, flew up in a streak from the ground. Maria's feet moved in time to the music; then, self-consciously, feeling that everybody must notice, she tried to alter her step. The sunlight and the crowds and the music held no interest for Mr. Burghclere, however; he pressed forward at a great pace. As they drew near St. Mark's, which still did not seem very much bigger, Maria saw that the pink and the gold and the blue were mosaics. For a moment they stood and stared at the façade, at the elaborate stonework, and the gilded pinnacles.

"And what is your opinion?" said Mr. Burghclere.

It was cruel of him, Maria thought, not to give her a hint as to what she *should* think. She hesitated. "It looks rather bright and gaudy. But perhaps it's just the sun."

To her relief, this did not seem to be a wrong answer. "Your instincts are sound, it is a little barbaric. But wait till you are inside."

And Maria and the grim attendant figure of Mrs. Clomper were hurried out of the sun and gaiety of the piazza into the cold shadows of the porch. The roof of the porch itself was full of mosaics. They were charmingly pretty, very much nicer than the huge ones on the façade. The trouble was there were so many of them, all telling some story that Maria could not immediately work out, and it made her neck ache as she peered up into the dimness of the roof. She would have liked to sit down at the base of one of the pillars and prop up her aching back while she looked. But she knew Mrs. Clomper would never allow this, and besides, Mr. Burghclere did not seem disposed to linger.

"Illustrations to the Book of Genesis," he remarked. "They require careful study. You can come back again with a Baedeker guide."

They left the cool shadows of the porch for the even cooler twilight of the church. Inside, it seemed much bigger, and thronged with people. Candles flickering on iron frames made pinpoints of light, and people wandered hither and thither over the immense floor, completely ignoring huddled figures of other people saying their prayers. Maria felt embarrassed, as though she ought not to be there at all. Surely one should not stare at buildings while other people were saying their prayers? But Mr. Burghclere paid them no attention either. He marched forward, pointing upward to this or that mosaic in the vaulting of the roof while Maria stumbled behind, bewildered and rather tired.

The mosaics he wanted her to see were high in the curves of the arches overhead. By craning her neck and standing in a certain place she could see part of it, to see the rest she would have to cross the floor and crane in a different direction. After a time Maria stopped looking and stood behind Mr. Burghclere where he could not see her and stared at the billowing floor.

It was stone, but it curved up and down in the most unaccountable way, like a petrified sea. Then she suddenly realized that St. Mark's was built on wooden piles, like the rest of the houses in Venice. The piles must be sinking; very soon the whole structure must collapse into the sea. Once she started thinking about this she could not stop. Wood could not last forever, especially when it was in water—and look at the weight these piles had to support! There seemed no reason why the whole vast structure should not collapse about their ears, and she stared around wildly, wishing Mr. Burghclere would hurry, wondering how all these people could move around so calmly.

She was biting her lip, and clenching her fingers into her hands, and fidgeting from foot to foot by the time Mr. Burghclere was ready to leave. The relief of leaving the chilliness and the dim light and emerging at last into the warmth and sunshine outside! It seemed like a different world, the sea sparkling on their left, the guitars strumming away around the cafés, the people strolling up and down so happily, the pigeons cooing. She drew a deep breath and hoped passionately that Venice was not just going to be mosaics and churches.

Mrs. Clomper Defied

The next day, however, there was no time for any churches in Venice itself. In the morning they had to move to the Palazzo Malipiero. They moved by boat, as Maria had seen the Italian family move the day before, only in this case there was, of course, no furniture. The gondolier took them across the Grand Canal to a small canal, taking his boat into it with the usual harsh shout of warning. They floated along between high, dark buildings and then emerged from this tunnel into a broader stretch of waterway which had a path running along one side.

Mr. Burghclere glanced up at a high stone wall that seemed to enclose a tiny garden. "Here we are. The Palazzo Malipiero. Exterior unimpressive, perhaps, but it is fine within."

The garden wall was broken by a tall gate that had

been painted black a long time ago but now was blistered and weather-beaten. There was a pierced iron grille in the top half, and the gate was approached by some steps that rose out of the water. Their gondolier jumped onto the top step and pulled the rusty chain of a bell that hung from the wall. Presently there was a shuffling sound inside and somebody struggled with bolts on the gate. When at last it opened they saw a bent, withered old woman who wore rusty black clothes. She stood and smiled at them with toothless gums, and her hands and her head trembled and shook. Mr. Burghclere said a few words to her in Italian, and she replied shrilly and with much gesturing. Then she led them all in.

Beyond the high wall and the prisonlike gate lay a tangled garden. Maria herself would hardly have called it a garden, for there was no grass, no flowers, just a patch of gravel, some ugly evergreen shrubs that had grown too tall and were fighting each other for light and space, and, in the middle, a small thicket of ivy out of which emerged the moss-covered head and shoulders of a female figure. The old woman had noticed Maria gazing about her.

"*Giardino*," she said, smiling and showing toothless gums. Then she pointed to where the statue struggled out of the ivy. "*Fontana. Bellissima!*" Her head wagged more violently than ever.

Mr. Burghclere noticed Maria's bewildered looks. "Garden," he said, "and fountain. Anna considers them very beautiful."

They went through the garden into an enclosed courtyard with a majestic stone staircase rising out of it. This they climbed, and at the top Anna held open a door with great pride.

"*Ecco. Appartamento signorile.*"

"The aristocratic quarters," said Mr. Burghclere. "Yes, I was fortunate in being able to rent these from Count Malipiero. This is the part of the building that the family keep for themselves. All their furniture and pictures are here. They have some quite fine things."

They were standing now in a gloomy stone passage that had a number of darkened pictures hanging on its walls. Maria looked around her. "Then is the rest of the house all empty?" she said timidly.

Mr. Burghclere was amused. "Empty, my dear Maria? Certainly not. On the ground floor we have, let me see, the Canonico Malipiero, an elderly clerical relation of the count. But he occupies only one room. There is also a Dalmatian family with an unspecified number of small children, and Anna herself, and some of her relations. On the mezzanine floor we have a German countess and an Italian family. On the *piano nobile*, here, ourselves. On the floor above us, and the floor above that, I don't now remember, though I seem to recollect some Armenians somewhere. But if you choose to investigate, you will find all their names beside the various bells downstairs. Space is very limited in Venice."

Mrs. Clomper made no comment at the time; she just pressed her lips together very tightly. But she had plenty to say later when she came to Maria in her bedroom.

"Nothing but a slum tenement, that's what it is," she said angrily, kneeling in front of Maria's portmanteau. "All those people crammed and stacked all around us. It's the first time I've been called upon to stay in a house that wasn't lived in by the family that owned it, I can tell you, Miss Maria. Call it a palace—why, it's no better than a piggery!"

"It's rather pretty though," said Maria. She too had been shocked at Mr. Burghclere's airy cataloguing of the various families squeezed around them, and she was trying to comfort herself as well as Mrs. Clomper. "Look at the ceiling!"

The ceiling was painted with nymphs and various floating female figures who had very little on. Mrs. Clomper looked up at it for a second with a grim expression. "Just what you might have expected. To think of such things being on *ceilings*—it's bad enough in statues. Well, Miss Maria, I tell you straight, I don't approve of such goings on and I never shall. And what really upsets me is Mr. Burghclere, who's as English as the rest of us, letting himself go in for it. What the poor dear warden would have said if he'd known that four weeks after he'd passed on, his niece would be sleeping with all these wicked pagan pictures in her bedroom, I just can't think." And Mrs. Clomper started lifting out clothes from the portmanteau and slamming them down on a nearby chair with much fury.

Maria tried to help, but it was clear that Mrs. Clomper did not wish her to, she wanted to be a martyr by herself. So Maria wandered around the room, inspecting the furniture, trying to peer through the shutters. The ceiling might be painted, but nobody had bothered very much about the walls. They were not even papered, just washed a dirty sage green, which showed up all the cracks and holes in the plaster. The furniture was heavy and ornate; marble-topped for the most part, which gave it a chilly look, and the bed was a huge four-poster, decked with threadbare faded brocade curtains.

It was hard work to push the shutters open. They were ill-fitting and two of the hinges had broken, but at last they gave way and the room was filled with sun. Maria gave a little shriek of pleasure. "There's a balcony outside," she called, and stepped out on to it. She found she was looking down at the little garden. From here the tangle was more pleasing, the high wall looked romantic, and there was a glimpse of the canal beyond.

She thought it might be very pleasant to sit here in the afternoons, reading and watching the canal, and the houses beyond it. She looked back into the room. Mrs. Clomper was still unpacking ferociously and, very boldly, Maria decided to wander around the apartments by herself.

Outside the bedroom it was very still. There was a chilly damp in the air, and it felt as though it was a very long time since the Malipiero family had occupied their palace. She went down the dark passage, paused by a double-leafed door, pushed it a little way, and peered in. She saw a huge room with a marble floor, and furniture ranged around the edges. The furniture might once have been very fine, but it was moldering and neglected now. The wood of the chests and commodes was warped and cracked; what once had been velvet and silk upholstery on the chairs was hanging in ribbons and faded to gray. The ceiling and walls were painted with the same sort of flimsily covered flying figures that Mrs. Clomper had objected to in Maria's room, and with swags and festoons of fruit and flowers; but these had faded too, and there were patches of damp on them.

Maria walked through the room to a double-leafed door on the far side. This led into another, smaller room of the same sort, and from there into more rooms, always with this air of decayed splendor, always leading into yet one more. Finally she reached what could only be a library. It was fairly small by the standards of some of the vast saloons she had just walked through; it was also very dark, the reason being that its only window looked out into the small courtyard in the heart of the palazzo.

Nevertheless, it was a beautiful room. On three sides the walls were lined with carved bookcases, with marble busts of ancient writers ranged on top of them. The books on the shelves were immense and bound in calf or vellum, and stood behind a brass latticework. Below the shelves were cupboards whose doors were inlaid with colored woods to make pictures of musical instruments, books, and globes. The only furniture in the room was a massive desk, two or three carved chairs with arms, and a pair of huge globes that stood on the floor, their map surface so yellowed and dark that very little could be seen on them. Maria had just seated herself in front of the desk, and was imagining herself a great scholar writing some work of profound learning, when she heard footsteps approaching over marble floors. Mr. Burghclere came in to find her standing guiltily by the desk.

"So you have found my sanctuary already. And how do you like it?"

"It's very nice. It reminds me of home, of Uncle Hadden's library, I mean."

"It will answer the purpose very well, I think, until

we get to the Villa Gondi. It means that I can do the work that I need to do here in privacy and seclusion without having to resort to libraries. Privacy, this is the thing. How I dislike having to rub shoulders with my fellow scholars! Even to say good morning to them in the libraries is exhausting. However, no work today, we are going to Torcello." Mr. Burghclere paused, and looked around him with a satisfied air. "I am glad you like my study. I doubt whether anything in it has changed since the seventeenth century. The Malipieri have been more given to the pleasures of the flesh than of learning."

Flesh: Maria was reminded of the pictures on her bedroom ceiling. "Mrs. Clomper doesn't like the flesh much," she observed diffidently.

Mr. Burghclere gave a bray of laughter and struck his hand on the desk. "Upon my word, I am sure she does not. Well said, Maria." He laughed so much that Maria felt she must too, out of politeness, though she was not sure what was so very funny, and in any case felt that she was in some way betraying Mrs. Clomper, whom, after all, she had known far longer than she had known Mr. Burghclere.

"Well," said Mr. Burghclere at last. "We go to Torcello this afternoon. I have ordered an early lunch so that Mario can take us to catch the two o'clock steamer."

They ate lunch in one of the rooms that Maria had already seen. It was not a proper dining room, but there did not seem to be such a room in the whole *appartamento*. Apparently you just pulled up chairs to a table and ate where you fancied. There were precious objects all around them, pictures, statues, florid furniture, and a vast, flamboyant chandelier of red and white glass above their heads, but the meal was served on coarse, cracked plates, and was not very good. It consisted of some lukewarm soup with bits of vegetable and rice floating in it, and then a piece of boiled beef. There were no vegetables, no dessert, just some cheese which Mrs. Clomper refused with a shudder. It certainly did smell very strong, and Maria could not bring herself to take any either.

"Does Anna cook for us?" ventured Maria, wondering whether it was because of her shaking hands that the food was cooked so badly.

"One of her daughters, Giovanna, I believe." Mr. Burghclere with relish spread an evil-smelling cheese on his roll. "The kitchen, of course, is down below on the ground floor."

Mrs. Clomper had a great deal to say about this when she came in to see that Maria was suitably dressed for the boat trip. "You'll need a lot of clothes, Miss Maria, so mind you, put them on. I don't know where we're going, I'm sure, but one thing is certain, it'll be on the water, there's no escaping from *that*. I don't know what we'll be dead from first, drowning or poisoning. I never tasted such rubbish as they gave us today. And on plates I'd be ashamed to offer to a kitchen maid! Stone cold, every morsel of it, and what's more, they hadn't even *tried* to warm the plates!"

"They have to carry it up from downstairs," said Maria apologetically.

"Such nonsense I've never heard," said Mrs. Clomper roundly. "They need someone to tell them what's what. The idea of carrying food up all those stone stairs, in a courtyard that's open to all the weather! They're nothing but heathen savages here, Miss Maria, I'll tell you straight, and the sooner Mr. Burghclere finds it out for himself, the better it'll be for us all."

When Mrs. Clomper had said that they would be out on the water, she obviously had not realized how much water there would be. Torcello turned out to be an island far out on the lagoon. Their gondolier took them across the Grand Canal, and they walked down a quayside from which Maria caught glimpses of the piazza where they had been yesterday, and the golden domes of St. Mark's. The little steamer which went to Torcello was moored by a delicious pink and white building, with lovely white stonework, ornate arches, and balconies.

"The Doges' Palace," said Mr. Burghclere in a bored way as though he knew it far too well. "We shall be coming to that, never fear, Maria. There is a fine Tintoretto, which it would never do to miss."

Mr. Burghclere led them to seats right in the bow of the little craft, presumably to be as far as possible from other people. They were just the seats that Maria would have chosen herself, but she knew that Mrs. Clomper, if she had to go on a boat at all, would at once make for cover, and she gave her nervous, sidelong looks. At first Mrs. Clomper said nothing; when the boat started she settled her outer clothes around her with the air of one who knows she is marching into the jaws of death but realizes it is useless to complain.

The steamer chugged slowly around the outskirts of Venice, past quarters that were not in the least romantic and often rather squalid. Mrs. Clomper stared fixedly ahead and not a muscle of her face moved. It was only when it became obvious that the boat was leaving the shores of Venice and was heading into the vast waters of the lagoon that she stiffened in her seat and spoke for the first time.

"Are we going out in all this?"

Mr. Burghclere had been idly turning over the pages of a book he had brought with him. He looked up now with a bland smile. "Certainly, unless you wish to be put down at San Michele yonder. We could always call for you a few hours later on our way back."

He was indicating some gray stone walls that rose sheer out of the water a little way ahead of them. Maria could see the tops of dark cypresses behind the walls, and the roof of what might be a chapel.

"It looks pretty," said Maria.

"I suppose it is quite pretty as Italian cemeteries go," remarked Mr. Burghclere. "Though Italian tombs are rather florid to the English taste. Do I take it that you wish to see the place too, my dear Maria?"

"Oh, no," said Maria with horror. She could not have explained just why she felt so horrified to discover that the island was a graveyard. She liked English graveyards. But there the dead were still part of the place where they had lived. Here they were shut away in the middle of the water, in a place that now seemed to her like a prison, behind huge, impenetrable walls, with great black doors that looked as though they opened only to take people in, never to let them out, and were approached by steps slimy and green from the water that lapped at them. Worst of all, she could see a long black boat moored by one of the doors. It had a low platform on it, and it could have been used only to bring a coffin. She shuddered and looked away.

It took her some time to drive the sinister island from her mind, and the boat had moved right out into the lagoon before she was aware of it. The water was very still. Lines of gnarled, seaweedy posts stretched out in front of them, there was a sand dune here and there with coarse tussocks of grass showing on it, an occasional small boat lying still on the water, fishing perhaps; and far, far off, rising from below the horizon, two church towers. The sky was not clear today, there were little clouds that looked like fish scales, but Maria loved the feel of the breeze in her face and the smell of sea.

The church towers came nearer. They passed islands that Maria thought surely must be Torcello, but they never were. Then an island larger than any they had passed loomed up, and this accounted for one of the towers.

"Burano," remarked Mr. Burghclere, lifting his head from his book. "We are nearly there." He surveyed the other passengers on the boat with a look of distaste. "I hope most of our companions descend here. Torcello is a place that one likes to oneself."

It seemed that Burano was the destination of everybody but themselves. Scrambling and pushing, laughing and chattering, the other passengers, who were all Italian, climbed onto the little quay, and the boat moved on. They reached Torcello a few minutes later. At least Mr. Burghclere appeared to recognize it and got to his feet, but all Maria could see was a dilapidated little wooden wharf and a winding muddy creek.

She felt almost frightened when she stood on the

bank and watched the boat turn around and chug slowly off into the distance, leaving the three of them abandoned on what seemed to be a desolate, flat waste in the middle of the waters. They walked slowly up a path that led by the side of the creek. Dirty brown little urchins were playing on its banks, and they looked around to hoot and shriek at the strangers. Two of them came gamboling up and held out dirty hands and shouted. Mr. Burghclere pushed his way past them, but Mrs. Clomper stopped and shook her skirts.

"Go away, you nasty little wretches!" she shouted in a voice that seemed trembling and hysterical. Maria, who had never known Mrs. Clomper otherwise than self-possessed and calm, was aghast. Then Mr. Burghclere turned and shouted threateningly at them, and the urchins scattered.

They had reached a bridge on the creek now. Ahead of them was a grassy space that had on it two crumbling churches, a tower that was one of those Maria had seen across the lagoon, a couple of houses, and that was all. Maria stared around her. She had expected a village at least, but there was nothing. She could not even think where the little boys lived.

"Is this all there is?" she asked.

"All that is left of it," said Mr. Burghclere. "It used to be a thriving little colony centuries ago. But the decay is singularly beautiful, do you not think?"

"Do you mean that this is all we have come to see?" said Mrs. Clomper shrilly. "All that way in that nasty boat just for this?"

Maria was horrified, Mrs. Clomper seemed to have lost all hold of herself. But Mr. Burghclere took it very coolly. "I think you are not yourself, Mrs. Clomper," he remarked. "Perhaps you would like to sit here and recover while Maria and I take a little stroll." He pointed out a large stone armchair that stood, in a surprising way, in the middle of tall grass, and then strolled off with an air of being completely unperturbed by the Mrs. Clompers of this world. Maria gave her a frightened, undecided look, and then pattered off, following him. After all, he had taken Uncle Hadden's place, so she supposed it was he that she should obey.

Together they walked over to the two churches, which lay side by side, with long grass and weeds growing around them, and with a general air of neglect and disuse. Mr. Burghclere led the way to the larger church, and there sitting on the porch was an old woman, the first human being Maria had seen on the island except for the boys. She was so old that she had shrunk almost to the size of a child, and so bent that her chin nearly touched the table she was sitting at. Her face was etched with a network of deep furrows, and her nose and her chin nearly met. She held out a shriveled hand for the money that Mr. Burghclere gave to her. Maria

was scandalized. To have to pay money to go into a church! Inside the church she was even more shocked, it was so desolate and spiritless. Here and there it even looked as though people had been digging in the floor.

"This is the ancient cathedral," said Mr. Burghclere. "It is not used now, I think. There are some fine mosaics. Look at the apostles in the apse, and there is an interesting Last Judgment behind you."

Dutifully Maria looked at the apostles standing on either side of the Virgin and Child. She rather liked the way their sandaled feet rested on mosaic daisies, though their faces looked very much the same to her eye. She turned to stare at the Last Judgment, which filled the whole of the wall at the back of the cathedral. There were hundreds of figures, and as Mr. Burghclere pointed out scenes, she screwed up her eyes and tried to see which he meant. Much of it represented Hell, and there were a great many demons tormenting people. Maria grew weary of looking and could think of nothing to say.

When they left the building the old woman on the porch had been joined by a sallow little girl who seemed to be racing four snails across the ledger in which Mr. Burghclere had signed his name. She glanced at them with complete lack of curiosity and went on prodding her snails. Mrs. Clomper was sitting forbiddingly in her stone armchair in the long grass. Mr. Burghclere glanced in her direction.

"One might say that the good Mrs. Clomper is a worthy occupant of the throne of Attila."

Maria was at a loss to understand. "Do you mean Attila, the king of the Huns?" she asked nervously.

"Attila the terrible, who swept over Lombardy and destroyed Torcello. They say that that is his throne." Mr. Burghclere waved toward Mrs. Clomper and the stone armchair.

Though Maria dutifully laughed at this learned joke, she felt rather ashamed of herself, and looked guiltily toward Mrs. Clomper. But the problem of whose side she should be on became exceedingly acute when they came out of the second church (it was even more crumbling and decayed than the first). Mr. Burghclere was telling her that she really must climb the *campanile* (as he called the high tower of the cathedral which Maria had watched on the horizon long before they ever reached Torcello).

He went to collect the key from the aged custodian, and was whirling it around his finger and describing to Maria the magnificent view she would see from the top; not only Torcello, but the whole lagoon on which Venice and the other islands lay, the open sea beyond, and the snow-covered peaks of the Tyrolean Alps. They were standing by the ivy-covered *campanile* (which stood quite separately from the cathedral, several yards away) when Maria suddenly heard Mrs. Clomper's voice at her shoulder and swiftly turned around. Mr.

Burghclere by this time had unlocked the door; it was warped and weatherbeaten and looked as though it had been knocked together from a few decaying planks.

"I hope, Miss Maria, you have not taken such leave of your senses as to go a-clambering around inside *that* place!" Mrs. Clomper pointed a trembling finger at the *campanile*. Maria looked imploringly at Mr. Burghclere, who came to her rescue.

"I propose to take Miss Maria to the top, certainly," he said smoothly. "There is a quite unequaled view up there."

"View or no view," said Mrs. Clomper hysterically, "no English young lady ought to go up there; let Italians and other nasty foreigners do as they please. And Miss Maria knows it as well as I do."

Mr. Burghclere shrugged and looked with raised eyebrows at Maria. She realized that the decision was left to her. If she obeyed Mrs. Clomper, Mr. Burghclere would have no further use for her; if she went up the *campanile*, Mrs. Clomper would never forgive her. She looked in an agony at Mr. Burghclere, saw his impatient frown, and went through the door he was holding open. After all, she could always apologize to Mrs. Clomper afterward; she felt she did not know Mr. Burghclere well enough to apologize to him.

The stairs were more dilapidated than she would have believed possible. The tower was nothing but a hollow shell, and the rickety wooden steps clung crazily to the walls all the way up. Maria, who had been expecting a stone spiral staircase, was appalled. But she could not retreat now. Giddily she fumbled her way up, trying never to allow her eyes to drop down to the fearful black depths at the bottom of the tower, and keeping as close to the walls as she could, for in places there was not even a handrail.

At last they emerged on a platform at the top, and then she knew that the climb, the defying of Mrs. Clomper, had really been worthwhile. Breathlessly she clung to her hat and stared around her. The lagoon lay still, like a pond. There were specks on it which must be boats, and nearer some boats with yellow sails that looked like a drift of butterflies. Below them the island spread out, the few houses that they had already seen, and then fields, cultivated like a market garden.

Beyond Torcello were more islands; Burano, closely set with houses, just over a narrow strait of water, then more islands, all flat and low in the water, some of them no more than sandbanks. And far away in the distance were domes and towers with the sun glinting on them. Venice. Maria sighed with pleasure and leaned on the wall. The wind ruffled her hair, but the sun was warm, so were the stones of the *campanile*, and she did not think she had ever been so happy. Even the unpleasantness of Mrs. Clomper's anger dwindled to a tiny speck.

She was still happy when she picked her way carefully down the tower. She would go and apologize and explain now to Mrs. Clomper, and say how wonderful it had been and really something she should not have missed. But Mr. Burghclere did not give her any opportunity. He looked at the ominous figure seated on the stone chair. "I sense thunder," he said lightly. "Let us explore the island."

Maria again felt guilty, but nevertheless, she had a delightful sense of being a fellow conspirator as she followed Mr. Burghclere. They walked down narrow paths through fields of what Mr. Burghclere told her were artichokes. Here and there was a man hoeing between the rows, straw-hatted, shirt-sleeves rolled up, but nobody they saw paused to look at them. With little cries of delight Maria bent down to look at the flowers by the path, small marigolds, deep blue grape hyacinths, tiny tulips.

Even in the boat coming back she was happy though she had not yet made her peace with Mrs. Clomper. She held her limp bundle of flowers and pressed them to her nose from time to time. Across the still waters Venice was approaching, in a golden haze from the setting sun, and for the moment she was perfectly happy.

Mrs. Clomper No More

The Palazzo Malipiero seemed very dark when at last they returned. By this time it was late, for the journey had taken a long time. But there was still light in the air, whereas inside everything was shadowy.

In a cowardly way, Maria took refuge in the library as soon as she had taken off her hat and coat. It was the only place where she was certain of being safe from Mrs. Clomper. She did want to apologize and explain, of course, but there was bound to be a long and wrathful scene, and surely it would be better not to start on this until after supper.

They all three of them had this meal together. Maria had never stayed up for a late dinner in England, and she supposed that Mrs. Clomper, if she had eaten such a meal, must have had it alone in the housekeeper's room. But here Anna could not be expected to serve three different meals at different times all through the evening, and a table was laid for the three of them in the little room where they had eaten lunch. There was a magnificent silver, branched candelabrum on the table, but the candles in it were all different lengths and were misshapen with gobbets of grease that had trickled down them. There was also a lamp on a marble-topped table at one side, but the room was dark and full of shadows and rather cold. Anna had brought up their first course and departed, leaving on the table a mound of what Mr. Burghclere said was *pasta*—short lengths of white wormlike food topped with a curl of butter and a blob of tomato sauce. Maria had dutifully struggled through hers—she had never been allowed to leave food on her plate. But Mrs. Clomper had refused to help herself to any, and the atmosphere was full of foreboding.

However, the trouble did not break until Maria had left the table to ring for Anna to bring up the second course. She was just coming back to her chair when she saw a mouse leap out of it. She was not particularly afraid of mice, but she was startled to see it jump from a chair where she had been sitting a minute before. She gave a little shriek.

"There's a mouse!" she called. It was difficult to see

in the bad light where the mouse had gone. But Mrs. Clomper, who had hastily risen, overthrowing her chair with a terrible clatter, gave a scream such as Maria had never heard before. "The nasty, horrid thing . . . my leg!" Then she clung to the table and screamed and screamed.

The fact that Mrs. Clomper had said anything so indelicate as "leg" was a certain sign, Maria knew, that she was almost out of her mind with terror. And the screaming was so dreadful too. Maria rushed up to Mr. Burghclere and shook his arm.

"What shall we do?" she shouted. "I think the mouse has run up her skirts."

Mr. Burghclere seemed completely unruffled, though he was frowning distastefully at the commotion. He broke a piece of bread from his roll. "Mice have strange ideas of comfort," he remarked.

In spite of her screams, Mrs. Clomper must have heard this. "You wicked, horrible—" she began exclaiming just as Anna burst into the room with a dish in her hand and loud cries of "*Mamma mia!*" and a torrent of Italian questions.

Mr. Burghclere looked around and said laconically, "*Un topo.*" Then he inspected the dish Anna had brought up.

It was left to Maria to try to explain, which she did in English, pointing to Mrs. Clomper's skirts, pointing to her own legs. Anna seemed to understand. At any rate, she took Mrs. Clomper's arm and led her from the room, chattering volubly while Mrs. Clomper gave shuddering gasps.

Maria hovered uneasily, not liking to sit down while Mrs. Clomper was in such trouble. "Do you think she will be all right?" she asked anxiously. "Do you think she will faint or something?"

"Let us not attempt to probe these feminine mysteries," said Mr. Burghclere dryly. "No, I should find another chair to sit in, Maria. There may be other mice and I do not want more hysteria. Can I help you to some ragout of veal?"

Maria did not see Mrs. Clomper until long after she had put herself to bed and blown out her candle. She was suddenly awakened by a light, and sitting up in alarm she saw a figure by her bed.

"Miss Maria," said Mrs. Clomper's voice, grim, as Maria had never before heard it. "I have just given Mr. Burghclere my notice. I have told him that I will stay here till the morning, but not a second longer. What I wish to know is whether you are going to come with me."

"You're going tomorrow?" Maria was wide awake now. "All by yourself?"

"Unless you are with me, Miss Maria. I have just told Mr. Burghclere that living in this piggery is one thing, and I would endure that, since it is my duty. But going out in boats, and being insulted and flouted at every turn, and having vermin swarming around me, that is quite another matter, and is more than flesh and blood can stand, as I told Mr. Burghclere a few minutes ago. But I have my duty to you to consider, Miss Maria, and I strongly advise you to come along home with me. Then we can see Mr. Josephs and make new arrangements."

Maria wrung the sheets in her anguish. "But I want to stay here!"

"Stay here in this sham palace where they can't even put a stitch of carpet on the floor, with those dirty Italians bringing you cold food all the time and jabbering their silly nonsense at you! Miss Maria, I give you solemn warning, you won't like it for long."

"But Mr. Burghclere said he was going to teach me Italian, and I think the palace is rather pretty really, and I loved going to Torcello and there's so much I want to see," wailed Maria. "Oh, Mrs. Clomper, do let me stay!"

"If you want to stay, there's nothing I can do, you're in Mr. Burghclere's charge. Though I tell you straight, Miss Maria, he's not fit to have charge of a canary bird, let alone a young lady. Mooning about pictures and churches all the time, with not a thought in his head for anybody's comfort or feelings. Besides, I shouldn't be in the least surprised if there isn't something wrong with every drain in the place—sorry as I am to have to say such a word. We'll all be down with fever before we know where we are."

"But I don't want to go away," moaned Maria. She felt a cold sweat breaking out on her back. She had thought she was so safe now from England and schools.

"Is that your last word?" said Mrs. Clomper harshly.

Maria twisted the sheets around her hand in a frenzy. "Yes, yes, I want to stay in Venice. And we won't be here so very much longer, we'll be going to the Villa Gondi, so it doesn't matter if these drains aren't very good. And Uncle Hadden's books will be going there too, and I do so want to see them again," she gabbled, trying to persuade Mrs. Clomper that she was not being willful and stupid, trying to persuade her to stay herself.

"Very well, Miss Maria. But I warn you, you'll repent it!"

And Maria was left to sleep. Next morning a pale, dark-eyed young girl brought in hot water. Maria washed and dressed and hung around in her bedroom, waiting for Mrs. Clomper, feeling it would not be polite to go in search of breakfast without her. Last night's dramatic dialogue seemed all a dream now. Mrs. Clomper would never abandon her and set off for England by herself.

When at last, tired of waiting, she wandered out of her room, she could find no signs of breakfast anywhere, no tablecloth or cups and saucers. She peered into the room where they had eaten that dramatic dinner the night before. There was no table laid there, only a few crumbs still scattered from the last meal. She wandered on through the rooms, but everywhere was lifeless and museumlike, and there was no sign of any human being. At last, greatly daring, she rang a bell rope, and five minutes later Anna came panting into the room.

"Breakfast?" said Maria timidly, not as a command but as a question.

"*Colazione, sì, sì,*" said Anna, nodding her head vigorously. "*Subito, signorina.*"

"Do you know where Mrs. Clomper is?" said Maria loudly and slowly.

Anna clearly did know where Mrs. Clomper was, for she broke into a torrent of explanations and much gesticulation. But Maria just looked woefully uncomprehending, and Anna slowed down. "*Signora—ferrovia,*" she kept saying, pointing out of the window. Maria had to pretend that she understood, otherwise this might have gone on forever, so she smiled faintly and nodded, and Anna, satisfied, left the room.

Breakfast was later brought up by another dark-eyed girl who seemed to be one of Anna's relations. It consisted of a huge cup of very milky coffee, rather cold, two rolls, and an immense quantity of apricot jam. The tray was laid for only one person, so Maria thought she had better begin without waiting for Mr. Burghclere or Mrs. Clomper. She nibbled her roll and thought angrily how unfair it was that she should be called to choose between Mr. Burghclere and Mrs. Clomper. Children ought not to have to decide these things for themselves. It was like playing Oranges and Lemons over something really serious. She was brooding and nibbling when Mr. Burghclere came in. She had not heard him coming and looked up guiltily.

"I didn't know what to do about breakfast," she said apologetically. "There didn't seem to be anybody about."

"That was quite right," said Mr. Burghclere vaguely. "I am glad you succeeded in finding somebody to bring it to you."

"Will Mrs. Clomper be coming?" Maria asked hesitatingly. She felt diffident about introducing the subject of Mrs. Clomper when Mr. Burghclere had plainly quarreled with her.

Mr. Burghclere pulled a slender gold watch from his waistcoat pocket. "By this time Mrs. Clomper will be halfway to Padua, near enough. Giuseppe reports that he saw her safely onto the train."

"Then she's gone!" Maria was stunned. It was dreadful that she and Mrs. Clomper had parted without a word of farewell, without a word of the apologies that Maria had all along intended to make.

"She insisted on going by the earliest train in the

morning. I cannot say I am sorry; her presence threatened all our comfort and peace of mind. Now, Maria, I tell you what I propose. I have some work that I wish to do for the next hour. If you will join me at ten o'clock in the library, we can settle down to some Greek and Latin, then lunch, and then at three o'clock go and look at some pictures. Oh, and by the way, you will need a maid now that Mrs. Clomper has left us. I have arranged with Anna for one of her granddaughters to look after you. And that way you will learn Italian too, for Battista can speak no English whatever."

When Mr. Burghclere had disappeared into the seclusion of his library, Maria wandered down the great stone staircase and out into the garden. She was still bemused by the shock of Mrs. Clomper's departure. Mrs. Clomper might have been a drag on her enjoyment of life in Italy, but she was her only link with England and the old life there, and without her she felt desolate and frightened. Besides, she felt guiltily that she had been disloyal, and the light way Mr. Burghclere had dismissed the whole incident troubled her. Poor Mrs. Clomper, doing the long journey all alone when she hated foreigners so much. And seen off, too, by Giuseppe, whom she distrusted as much as any of them.

Maria went down the short gravel walk to the gate with its grille. She could peer through the rusty iron scrolls at the canal beyond. There were men bailing water out of a barge and calling cheerfully to each other, and on the other side of the canal she could see some small houses with old, old women sitting in upright chairs in the doorways, staring out blankly, their hands folded in their laps.

But she presently grew weary of the scene and turned and walked around the garden. It did not look as though sun ever reached it, it was so small and hemmed in by high walls. Under a cascade of ivy she found a lichened stone seat. For a moment she thought of bringing a book and reading there, but she decided against it. It would be so dreary to sit in that tangle of ivy and struggling evergreens. Besides, it was cooler today, the sky was cloudy with only a few patches of blue, and there was a chill breeze. So she walked back to the staircase and hesitated, her hand on the smooth cold stone of the balustrade. Behind closed doors down the dark passages that led from the courtyard she could hear people's voices. There seemed to be quantities of people in the house all busy and happy except her, and the thought of it made her feel sad and lonely.

Then a door opened and somebody came out, still talking cheerfully. It was Anna, and when she saw Maria she said "*Ah, signorina,*" and then a great deal more in very fast, shrill Italian. Maria just shook her head helplessly. Anna seemed to be beckoning her in somewhere, so she followed, and found herself in a vast stone-flagged kitchen. A fire was burning in a stone hearth built far out into the room, and over it pots dangled from a long crane. Huge cookery implements hung on the walls, and even huger stone jars stood all around the floor. Maria's first thought was that it was an illustration of an ogre's kitchen in a fairy tale, and her second thought that it was no small wonder the food was so cold and tasteless if it was prepared in this huge cavern with cooking implements like garden tools.

Then she noticed the people, and shrank back. There seemed to be so many of them, all sitting around a large table in the shadows, and all staring at Maria. She supposed they were Anna's relations; Mr. Burghclere had spoken of them. Confused, she moved toward the door. But Anna stopped her. "Battista," she called shrilly, and the slender, dark-haired girl whom Maria had met earlier that morning stood up and smiled diffidently.

This, then, must be the maid who was to replace Mrs. Clomper. A greater contrast you could hardly find. Battista would never stop Maria climbing up towers; it was difficult to see how either of them would ever understand a word the other said. Maria did not know what to say. She just muttered "How do you do," and Battista bobbed a sort of curtsy. Then Maria fled, leaving Anna and her crew of relations to discuss her loudly, she was certain of that.

As she ran down the passage toward the courtyard, she heard the Dalmatian family, or whoever it was that lived down here, quarreling stormily. From behind a closed door came crashings of furniture, a man's voice in anger, and children shrieking. She ran even faster, and nearly knocked over a mild, bespectacled little man in a long black cassock who came around the corner peering shortsightedly at a book and murmuring to himself. He did not even look up as she swerved away from him. This must be the old clergyman, the Canonico Malipiero that Mr. Burghclere had mentioned.

Once upstairs, she wandered in the huge saloons of the *appartamento signorile* until it was time to go to the library. She had dreaded her first lessons with Mr. Burghclere, but in fact they went well. It was odd how sometimes when you were translating everything was easy, all the words you wanted were on the tip of your tongue, and how other times you could stare baffled at a sentence without the remotest idea of even which end you should start. Today was one of the easy days, and Mr. Burghclere, though he said little, seemed pleased with her. She came to the end of the Horace ode that she had been translating, and gave a little sigh of pleasure.

"I wonder how many people have sat here and read. It's such a beautiful room for reading in."

"Not many of recent years, I fancy. The present male

members of the Malipiero family spend more time duck shooting on Torcello than reading their ancestors' books."

"And what about the family before them?"

"Oh, they went in for balls and ridottos and so on. You can see pictures of the sort of thing all round the other rooms. A very gay, butterfly-headed lot they were, the eighteenth-century Malipieri."

"But what about the people who bought these books?" Maria persisted.

"Ah, yes, that was in the days when learning really mattered, three hundred years ago or more. What was more, women had the same education as men. It was thought desirable that women should be witty and learned, not merely burdened with senseless accomplishments. That is what I have in mind for you."

"For me?" Maria was flattered that Mr. Burghclere should have any plans for her.

He nodded. "You already have a fair grasp of two ancient languages. You need to be fluent in Italian, and have a sound grasp of Italian culture, painting, architecture, and so on. Do you play any instrument?"

"Not very well," said Maria doubtfully, remembering her French governess's exhausting struggles to teach her to play the piano.

"No matter, an understanding of the theory of music is of far more importance than mere agility with the fingers. There are plenty of music masters in Italy. I will see about engaging one. You may be able to sing, of course. You have met Battista? A few weeks with her and you will be conversing fluently. Meanwhile, here is an Italian grammar to help you along, and Burckhardt's *History of the Civilisation of the Renaissance in Italy*. A year or two of this, and we will have you as well educated as a Renaissance princess—as Vittoria Colonna herself."

Pictures and Rain

*W*hen Maria took the two books from Mr. Burghclere she felt giddy with excitement at the vista that lay ahead of her. How wonderful to spend her time learning about things like architecture and painting and Italian instead of plodding away at the detestable subjects they made you take at school. She peeped into the Italian grammar and into Burckhardt and they both seemed fascinating, and quite easy. But she did not have a chance to look at them properly until much later, for the afternoon was given up to looking at pictures.

There seemed to be enough pictures in Venice to stock the galleries of all Europe—and nearly all of them by Bellini or Tintoretto. Maria, peering dutifully up at the masterpieces that Mr. Burghclere pointed out to her above ornate altars, wondered a little wearily how Bellini or Tintoretto could possibly have found time to have painted all they were supposed to have painted. She turned her head this way and that, screwing up her eyes and trying to pierce the bad light (the churches were always so dark) and see all the things Mr. Burghclere said were there.

They visited some three or four churches, and Maria had grown rather tired of them, and also of trying to stifle her yawns. She had begun a yawning fit which she could not stop, and it was exhausting trying to swallow her gapes. So she was pleased when Mr. Burghclere said that they would finish up with the Doges' Palace. They were walking today, so that Maria could see more of Venice, but Mr. Burghclere pressed forward at a great rate and in fact she saw very little.

Hurrying to keep up with him, she wished she could linger and look into the windows of the little shops, and turn around and stare at the street traders. Everything was so absorbingly different from England. She caught glimpses of milkwomen with broad straw hats and dangling earrings, carrying straw-filled baskets carefully packed with bottles of milk, of fishermen with shallow baskets of fish on their heads and under either arm, bargaining at the doors with aproned women who argued shrilly. She even saw one chopping up an eel on the doorstep, closely watched by a housewife with a tribe of children clinging to her skirts.

But Mr. Burghclere took no interest in such things. He marched forward relentlessly, without saying a word, merely sighing a little wearily when the wide skirts of ladies passing in the opposite direction made him squeeze back against a wall.

Once out of the shelter of the narrow passages and in the vast spaces in front of St. Mark's, it was very cold. There was an icy wind that made Maria press her arms close to her, when she was not holding on to her hat. Mercifully there were to be no mosaics today; they passed St. Mark's and went into the Doges' Palace just beyond it. Here they toiled up a vast staircase and went through room after room full of gold and painted ceilings, and pictures of the sort that Mrs. Clomper would have disapproved of. Maria grew so weary that she no longer attempted to tip back her head and examine the ceilings. Her yawning returned, and this time she did not trouble to smother it.

"Well?" said Mr. Burghclere at last with a question in his voice. It caught Maria off her guard. She had not expected her opinion to be asked. Also, she was in the middle of a yawn.

"I think it looks rather vulgar," she said shortly.

But Mr. Burghclere was delighted. Maria had never seen him so enthusiastic. He told her repeatedly on the way home that she was possessed of a fine natural taste, that most children of her age would have been impressed by all the gilt and splendor, and Maria quite forgot the tedium of the afternoon and walked back, light of foot, enchanted with Mr. Burghclere's opinion of her.

There was plenty of opportunity after that for the Italian grammar and the civilization of the Renaissance. In fact, she had the whole of the rest of the evening and a great deal of the succeeding days to devote to them, for except when she was out sightseeing with Mr. Burghclere or reading with him, she was left to herself. Obediently she tried to grapple with the principles of Italian, or to digest the facts about the despots of the fourteenth and fifteenth centuries, but she did not make much headway.

She used to wander through the empty rooms, looking for somewhere to work, settling herself in one slippery silk chair after another and never finding anywhere to her comfort. Many of the rooms were dark. On one side of the house they faced over the tangled little garden and the canal beyond, but the more important ones looked inward, onto the courtyard. And it was all so silent, not even the clocks ticked, and the merry sounds of Anna and her relations, the more strident noises of the Dalmatian family quarreling, never reached her up here.

Sometimes she wandered down into the garden. There she pressed her face to the grille and stared out at the canal beyond. It occurred to her that she must look like a prisoner gazing out at a world he could not reach, and she felt gloomier than ever. Nobody else ever came out here, in spite of the many families who were said to inhabit the *palazzo*. The only person she ever saw was the aged Canonico whom once or twice she met pacing up and down the path with what seemed to be a prayer book held close to his eyes. Up and down he walked with a flutter of his cassock as he turned, but so deep in his prayers that he never noticed there was anybody else in the garden at all.

The only time the *palazzo* came to life was immediately after the midday meal. Then, if you were near the staircase you could hear a tremendous sound of chattering, singing, concertina playing, shouting, coming from the windows that overlooked the courtyard. Maria did not know whether she liked or hated it; it made the gloomy rooms of the *appartamento signorile* seem drearier and emptier than ever. In any case, it soon stopped, and the families seemed to sink into torpor. They probably needed to sleep off the effects of their horrible *pasta*, Maria thought crossly. She considered the Italian food quite dreadful; always mountains of white worms, and an unending succession of tasteless veal dishes smothered in tomato. She felt dull and out of sorts and always seemed to have a lingering headache.

And all the time she wished and wished that there were somebody to talk to. It was the first time in her life that she had wanted company, and as she wandered through the vast rooms, the refrain of an old Scottish ballad went around and around in her head: "And still she sat, and still she reeled, and still she wished for company." But company, it seemed, was the last thing that Mr. Burghclere desired for himself. He seemed to have a morbid horror of people. He frowned and looked impatient if he found them in the places that he was visiting, and although he spoke to Maria in an airy way of the various noble Venetian families that he knew, he made no attempt to visit them.

For her part, she longed to see how Italian families lived, and to go inside their houses, but it seemed she was never going to be given the chance. There was somebody called Dr. Mula whom Mr. Burghclere several times seemed to be on the point of visiting. He had a high opinion of him. "A most distinguished man, of Jewish origin. Quite unlike the English physicians. In fact, I would go so far as to say that he is one of the most cultivated and widely read men I have met." They often passed Dr. Mula's house, and Mr. Burghclere every time would hesitate and look up, but he could never, it seemed, quite make up his mind to call.

Two or three days after Mrs. Clomper had left, Maria

was leaning her head against the glass of a window and looking up at a window across the courtyard, on a higher floor. She often stared at this window, it had a bird cage hanging outside in which a goldfinch fluttered its wings and sang. Maria thought drearily that she was rather like that bird, only her cage was so much larger, and she did not in the least feel like singing. She sighed. It must have been a loud sigh, for Mr. Burghclere, who had suddenly appeared at the far end of the room, heard it.

"Is there anything wrong, Maria?"

She scrambled to her feet, blushing guiltily. "Oh, no, thank you."

"You look a little pale. I wonder if you are getting enough exercise."

"Oh, yes, thank you," said Maria, remembering how her feet had ached with tramping over the marble floors of churches the day before.

"Still, perhaps you are short of fresh air. Let me see, tomorrow is Sunday. I shall have to spend the day looking through some manuscripts. I shall ask Battista to take you for a good English walk, and you can practice your Italian. How is it getting on, by the way?"

"All right, thank you." Maria prayed Mr. Burghclere would ask no more, for every day she found she had forgotten the grammar she had toiled over the day before, and conversation with Battista consisted mostly of signs, or else Maria spoke loudly and slowly in English.

So next morning Battista took Maria for her "good English walk." Mr. Burghclere did not seem to intend to go to church—of course, there might not even be an English church in Venice—and after breakfast he retreated to the library. She felt very desolate with this last fragment of her English routine taken from her, for she had never before been free to go for a walk at ten o'clock on a Sunday morning. Maria joined Battista in the courtyard, and they went through a back door into an alley outside the *palazzo*. The air was full of bells, but they did not peal as church bells pealed in England; they seemed pulled at random, and the sounds clashed and jarred.

The wind was cold, so they walked briskly, Maria did not know where. They pattered down alleys and passageways, always with the sound of their own footsteps following them—along canals, over bridges, into squares dominated by large churches. These were usually thronged with people in their best clothes hurrying into church, or, more leisurely, pulling on their gloves and strolling away from a service. Maria envied them. They had their churches to go to; she was thousands of miles from her own.

At last they emerged by the Grand Canal, where the wind blew keener than ever, cutting into them. There was a vast church here. Maria remembered having seen it from the other side of the canal.

"*Santa Maria della Salute*," said Battista, glancing up

at it. It was the first word she had said that morning. "*Ecco San Marco.*" She pointed across the canal. The wind lashed at them and blew their skirts close to them. There was rain in it now, and it stung Maria's face. She gazed across the canal. The big bell of St. Mark's was tolling. Only it was nothing like the bells of the Oxford churches. This was a deep, harsh note that clashed across the water. "Dong," it said, and then after a second or two, "dong." Tears came into Maria's eyes. In Italy they could not even ring bells properly. And she longed for England, for Oxford, the bells, the gardens that would be so green just now; the university parks. Why, she had not seen a tree that she could call a tree since she arrived in Venice. Surely even in Venice there must be a park somewhere. She turned to Battista.

"Isn't there a park in Venice?" But Battista looked quite blank. In her despair Maria remembered the word Anna had used the first day they had arrived at the Palazzo Malipiero. "*Giardino,*" she said pleadingly. But Battista paid no attention. She was shivering and looking up at the sky. "*Pioggia,*" she said, and pulled Maria's arm.

So they went back. The rain became much heavier before they reached the *palazzo*, and they arrived very wet. But during the next week it grew heavier still, for as far as Maria could tell, it never stopped, not for five minutes on end, for eight or nine days at least. There were times when it slackened a little and the sky looked lighter, and the clouds seemed higher, and at first, thinking of England, she imagined that it was beginning to clear up. But soon the clouds would gather again and the rain would take on a new energy. She gave up looking for it to clear during the day, though each evening she hoped that when she woke in the morning she would find blue skies. But before she drew back the shutters and looked out, before she opened her eyes even, she would know that nothing had changed. She could hear the water pouring out of the broken gutters and splashing into the little garden below.

Mr. Burghclere did not seem put out. "One can never be certain of the weather in Venice in the spring," he remarked. "We were fortunate to get those few sunny days. Besides, the weather hardly affects us. All that we want to see is so close. And we have our intellectual resources, have we not?"

But the weather did affect Maria. For one thing, it was so bitterly cold, and when you are living in a huge, marble-floored palace with nary a fireplace, or even a carpet, it is extremely hard to keep warm. The only time she ever managed to forget the misery of her numbed feet was during her morning lessons with Mr. Burghclere, when the anxiety of not disgracing herself (and also the interest of what she was reading) took her mind off everything else. Mr. Burghclere did not seem to mind Italian cold, although he had protested about English winds. He sat with his feet on a low velvet-covered stool with a rug about his knees. He told Maria that they were fortunate not to be living higher up in the *palazzo*, as the rain would most certainly be coming through the roof. "The only form of heating that the Venetians recognize is the sun," he said, drawing his rug more closely around his knees. "I hope you always sit with your feet on a cushion these days, my dear Maria."

Maria did try wrapping her feet in cushions, and she stripped the counterpane off her bed and put it around her. But it was no good, the cold drove into the very marrow of her bones. And there was hardly more comfort in bed, with icy sheets, and her feet like slabs of marble.

If it was cold in the house, it was far worse outside. Mr. Burghclere might say that everything in Venice was near, but even so, and with the gondola to take them most of the way, it was possible to get very wet. The rain and the wind drove at them, Maria's boots were thin, and, as she learned at once, not in the least watertight, and her feet were permanently sodden.

Passively following Mr. Burghclere, she tramped over acres and acres of marble floors of huge, cold churches, squelching out water at every footstep, able to think of nothing but her frozen feet. She no longer had the energy to take any interest in pictures. Indeed, she felt hatred for them all, for the bareness and the emptiness of the vast churches, for the floors that made her feet so cold, for the painters who had poured out all these pictures that she was being made to look at.

She remembered one church with particular loathing. It looked like a tablecloth, or, rather, a series of gigantic tablecloths. It was full of marble carved to look like drapery, and the white marble of the columns and pulpits were inlaid to imitate damask linen. They had come to see Tintoretto's "Martyrdom of St. Lawrence," and Maria could only rouse herself from her stupor of misery and cold to envy the saint for the warmth he must have on his gridiron.

All the time that they lingered inside the churches, Maria could hear the water streaming off gutters and falling from the heights of the roofs onto the stones below with great noise and force. The Venetians seemed never to have been told that there were such things as drainpipes, so unless you took care, the water from the roofs fell on you as you passed below. In any case, your legs would be soaked from the force of it bouncing off the pavement. Worst of all was the knowledge that when you got home you would be no warmer, that you would climb wearily up the great stone staircase with the rain beating down upon you, into rooms that were as cold as any church. Anna, who had to clamber up and down the stairs in the rain with their trays of food, showed no signs of minding the weather at all. "*Brutto tempo*," she would remark cheerfully as she set down a tepid dish of *pasta* in front of them. Or "*Sempre la pioggia*."

On one particularly horrible day, which Maria was to remember as long as she lived, Mr. Burghclere took her to see some pictures that he told her enthusiastically were the greatest in Venice. They were difficult to appreciate, he said, but he felt that Maria was now ready for them. It was unbelievably wet that day, the rain was falling more heavily than it had yet, and as they ran over the cobbles from the gondola to the *Scuola di San Rocco* (this was what Mr. Burghclere called the building), the rain nearly blinded them. It poured down Maria's face so that she shut her eyes, and by doing so walked right into the waterfall that was cascading off the roof of the *scuola*. She felt it go right through her hat and down her neck.

The *scuola*, so Maria was told, had once been a hospital for which Tintoretto had painted his greatest pictures. You certainly never would have known that it had ever been used for such a purpose. It looked like a church. It had an altar at one end, there was an enormously high ceiling, quantities of gold paint, and the walls were hung with the vastest, blackest paintings that Maria had yet seen. Mr. Burghclere was gazing at them with an awe and ecstasy that made Maria suddenly feel furiously angry. The light was so bad she could hardly see the horrible things, except as a sea of black. Yet Mr. Burghclere was examining the first canvas with rapt attention and pointing out details she was sure nobody could see, and if he was going to devote the same attention to each, they would be in this dreadful place till night fell, for there were at least a dozen more along the walls, to say nothing of a huge staircase that very likely led to more and yet more pictures.

She refused even to look up. She stared stubbornly at the floor and made no reply to Mr. Burghclere's comments, trailing wearily after him when he moved up a few yards to the next canvas. Her legs ached, her back and her neck ached, but there was nowhere to sit down except one chair near the man who took the money by the door. She turned her back on the pictures and stared longingly at it, and at the man, who had a little earthenware pot on the floor beside him, full of hot charcoal, which he was crouching over.

If only I could just warm my fingers! Maria thought, pressing them against her icy cheeks, and then, in her despair, trying to suck them warm in her mouth.

"Maria!" called Mr. Burghclere suddenly from some distance away. She jumped around guiltily. "Why, child, whatever are you doing?" he said rather testily.

Maria advanced toward him with a hanging head. "I'm just so very cold," she said in a faltering voice.

There were tears in her eyes and her lips were trembling.

"One is cold at first, naturally. But one soon forgets about it."

"I can't," said Maria almost defiantly. "I'm too wet."

"There seems very little purpose in continuing here, then," said Mr. Burghclere coldly. "We had better make our way back to the gondola."

So they left the cold gloom of San Rocco for the rainstorm outside. Maria was so numbed with cold and misery that she stepped under the waterspout again and was drenched for the second time. Her clothes and her shoes made pools on the black wood of the gondola, and she tried to wipe the rain out of her eyebrows and hair so that it would not run down into her eyes. Not a word was said as the gondola moved slowly through the maze of canals. Then suddenly Mr. Burghclere clapped his hands.

"We will go and call upon Dr. Mula," he said with the air of one who had made up his mind to undergo an unpleasant operation.

Maria was so cold and wet that she was beyond caring what happened. There was no point in wishing to go home; there was no warmth there. The main thing was that they were out of San Rocco. Above her head the rain drummed noisily on the roof of the gondola, and through the window she could see Mario standing by the side of the canal, bareheaded, his hand on his hip, carrying on a conversation with some woman who was talking to him shrilly out of the window of an upper floor room. Then he came back to the gondola and helped them out.

Like everybody else in Venice, Dr. Mula seemed to occupy only a room or two in the house where he lived. Mr. Burghclere led the way up a dark staircase where the walls were unpapered, the plaster crumbling, and here and there a banister missing. Two or three floors up Dr. Mula was standing at an open door. He greeted Mr. Burghclere with much enthusiasm. But what roused a flicker of interest in Maria was the acrid smell of smoke. Perhaps Dr. Mula had a stove!

There was indeed a stove in the room where they were shown. It was a monstrously large one, not the least like any stove she had seen before. It was built of bricks and plastering, whitewashed and painted outside, and it was filling the room with clouds of smoke. But it was the only sort of heat Maria had seen for the whole of this terrible, frozen week, and she advanced on it, holding out her hands.

Dr. Mula laughed. Though he had greeted Mr. Burghclere in Italian, he spoke to her in French, with the sort of accent Maria could understand, quite unlike the rapid chatter of French people. *"Vous avez froid?"*

She nodded and crept nearer the fire. And there she

stayed the whole time, thinking of nothing else but how, at last, she had found somewhere to thaw her frozen hands. She longed to take off her wet boots and hold her feet out to the warmth, but this, of course, was out of the question. She took in very little else except the fire. She noticed that Dr. Mula's untidy room was stacked with books, that he looked like a kind sort of man with a big nose and a fringe of thick gray hair around his polished bald head. Then it was time to go, and she followed Mr. Burghclere down the rickety stairs and out into the rain again.

In later years she remembered only a few moments of the day that followed, but she remembered them with painful vividness. She could recall how ill she felt when she woke, and the effort and determination needed even to sit up in bed. Battista, who was helping her dress, appeared to notice nothing, and Maria recalled how passionately she longed for Mrs. Clomper to come in and order her back into bed.

The other memory that remained with her was of sitting at the desk in the library. Her hands and feet were frozen, but her head was hot, and seemed to be floating, balloonlike, above her body. Her chest felt as though it were being hacked into fragments by red-hot knives. The words on the page in front of her made no sense at all, and she could not have told whether they were Latin, Greek, or Italian. She could hear Mr. Burghclere's voice expounding, reading, explaining, but his words made no sense either. He urged her impatiently to collect her wits and begin again. But it was no good, her wits were not there. He was waiting, the silence was terrible, she would have to say something. "Odysseus," she began because she really thought she had seen the word somewhere there on the page. But then even in her fuddled state she realized they were not reading Homer at all, it was Virgil's *Georgics* that she had in front of her.

"Maria!" said Mr. Burghclere, thumping his fist on the table. But by a great act of mercy he had not time to say more, for Anna poked her head around the door, said something very rapidly, and then ushered someone in.

Maria slumped back in her chair. By now she was capable of thinking only in terms of minutes, and for the next few moments she knew she was safe, for Mr. Burghclere was talking animatedly to the visitor whom she was vaguely aware must be Dr. Mula. Then for a second she was able to think clearly. Now would be the moment to escape from the library, now, while Mr. Burghclere was too occupied to remonstrate. She pulled herself to her feet and tried to make her way to the door. But her legs were trembling and it was difficult to guide them, and Mr. Burghclere's footstool was their downfall. She knocked it flying along the smooth glass of the marble floor, and just before she crashed to the ground after it, she saw, in a sudden flash, the startled faces of Mr. Burghclere and Dr. Mula, both staring at her.

Letters

After that Maria was no longer aware of the cold. In fact, she was aware of very little, she could hardly tell the difference between dreams and reality. From time to time she would see faces bending over her, a man's face—Dr. Mula, perhaps?—the head of a nun who seemed to be nursing her, washing her, giving her drinks; Mrs. Clomper, stern and forbidding, warning her about the drains; Harriet's face, anxious and pleading. But which of these were real and which were fantasy she did not know, nor did she care.

And sometimes all the faces became obliterated by a terrifying feeling that she was lying on the platform of that sinister black boat she had seen the day they went to Torcello. Ahead of her, gray walls rose sheer out of the water of the lagoon, and in the wall was a black gate that was edging open, inch by inch. She could see bony white fingers coming through, and the water lapped at stained green steps. "Stop!" she would try to shriek. "I'm not dead." But no sound would come out of her lips, and though she strained to move, her whole body seemed to have been turned to stone.

She had no idea how long she spent like this. It might have been weeks, it might have been days, but when one day she opened her eyes and saw sunlight in the room, and in the shadows a nun sitting, moving her lips over a little book, she knew without any difficulty that this was real, and that Harriet's face, Mrs. Clomper's face, the fearful vision of the cemetery island, had been dreams. At first she was perfectly content to lie there, spreading her hands on the coverlet and feeling the sun hot on them, staring up at the nymphs bounding over the clouds on the ceiling, or at the cracks on the sage-green paint of the walls.

But as she grew stronger she became more restless. Before, she had only the energy to think of the warmth of the sun on her hands, of the wall opposite her bed, but now her mind was able to move beyond what she could see from her pillows. And she began to think of all the water that lay around them, underneath them. Of how the house was supported only on wooden piles, probably seaweedy and rotten, of how the floors of St. Mark's rose and fell like billows, and of how any moment a pile might give way and the whole house would crumble into the ooze and slime. The more she thought about it, the more impossible it seemed that the house could stand for a day longer.

Then one day when she woke she was certain the cracks on the wall had grown longer, and she shrieked. The nun who sat in her room day and night and who nursed her so silently and efficiently that Maria hardly thought of her as a person, came over, startled. She spoke to Maria. But Maria could not understand. It was this that made her cry, the feeling that she was surrounded by uncomprehending foreigners, that there was not a soul within a thousand miles who could speak a language that she could understand.

She was still crying when Dr. Mula came in. He stood at the foot of the bed and smiled at her and asked her in bad French what the matter was. Maria did not speak French well enough to explain to him. Besides, he was a foreigner too, so she just stared at him through her tears.

"*Qu'y a-t-il?*" said Dr. Mula again.

Maria struggled to think of something that she could put into French. "*L'eau,*" she said feebly at last. "*Trop de l'eau. L'eau partout.*" And she made feeble gestures with her hands.

Dr. Mula rumbled with laughter. He was leaning against one of the bedposts, and Maria could feel the bed shaking. Even the nun, who was standing unobtrusively in the shadows, smiled gently.

"*Eh bien, vous n'aimez pas Venezia?*" said Dr. Mula.

It seemed rude to say she did not like it. Maria struggled again to find French words. "*Il pleut toujours,*" she said pleadingly. "*Et il fait froid.*"

"*Mais maintenant le soleil brille.*" Dr. Mula pointed to the sunbeams that came in through the half-closed shutters.

"*Maintenant,*" said Maria, "*mais . . .*" Here she stopped. She had wanted to say that it might be sunny now, but soon the rain was sure to come again and she could not bear the sight of any more rain or any more water. She was sure she would go out of her mind. But this was far beyond her command of French, and anyway, she was too tired to think of the simplest words. So she sighed wearily and lay back on her pillows again.

That evening Mr. Burghclere came to visit her. She had seen very little of him while she was ill. Indeed, there had been a time when she had forgotten such a person existed. Lately, since she had been better, he had appeared at the door morning and evening, looked in nervously, and said, "Good morning, Maria" (or "good evening"). "I trust you are feeling better." To which Maria invariably replied, "Yes, much better, thank you." Whereupon Mr. Burghclere with a look of relief would hasten away.

But this time he came right into the room. The nun

brought him a chair and he sat down by Maria's bed. Maria twisted her fingers apprehensively and stared at the two little hillocks that her feet made near the bottom of the bed. Mr. Burghclere gave a little cough.

"Dr. Mula tells me that you are eager to leave Venice."

This sounded as though Maria had been complaining, and she flushed and tried to excuse herself. But Mr. Burghclere waved her apologies and explanations aside.

"We have of course been unfortunate with the weather. Spring is always chancy in these north Italian towns, especially in Venice, which is so near the mountains. Perhaps I made a mistake staying so long. But I wanted to show you some of the glories of Venetian art. However, as soon as you are fit to travel we shall go to Feronia. It is the ideal place for convalescence, plenty of sun and warmth, and Florence not too far away when you are ready to look at pictures again."

Pictures! Maria shuddered at the thought. She remembered those vast black canvases in San Rocco and she wanted to shriek with despair. She decided at that moment that she would never allow herself to be well enough to see pictures again, even if she had to stay a helpless invalid for the rest of her life. But on the other hand, she did want to leave Venice. She was aching to see trees and grass, even if only from a window, and to have earth below her, not water. So she did get better.

Dr. Mula and Suora Imelda (the nun who nursed her) were surprised and pleased at how soon she was able to sit up in a chair, to walk for a few halting steps around her room. It made her feel weak and giddy, but she drove herself to do it, as she also drove herself to eat the soups and morsels of meat that Anna sent up. She would do anything to get away from Venice, and as soon as she got to Feronia and the Villa Gondi she would relapse again, she had made up her mind to that.

And so the time came when Dr. Mula agreed she was fit to make the long journey. Battista packed her clothes, and the room became empty and anonymous, as though she had never occupied it. The night before they left she could hardly sleep for worrying about the traveling that lay ahead of her. There seemed so many hazards, so much to be endured before she could ever lie comfortably in a bed again, and she twisted and turned as she thought of them all. Even supposing there was a bed at all! Things might be worse at the Villa Gondi than they were here, and in Feronia she would be still farther away from England.

But when the next day came she no longer worried about matters like these, for the journey was so long and seemingly so endless that she was too tired to think about anything. Her only ambition now was to find somewhere to lie down, and once she had, she vowed she would never get up again. During the early part of the journey the train rushed through flat, flat fields, divided up by ditches. Maria closed her eyes wearily, but every time she opened them to see whether the landscape had changed, she always found it the same, fields and fields and fields and not even a hedge, just sometimes a few willows and perhaps a dirty, tumble-down farm.

Then they changed trains, and she had to endure the hubbub of a large station and shrieking engine whistles and hustling crowds. Battista and Suora Imelda were very kind. They wrapped rugs around her knees, they tried to tempt her with cups of broth, they put cushions behind her head. But all she wanted was that this horrible, racketing journey should be over so that she might lie down and sleep. Then the train started up again, and soon they were among mountains, climbing up wearily, plunging into long tunnels.

She must have fallen asleep at last, because she found herself being gently shaken awake and helped down onto the platform of a station. Mr. Burghclere was there, assuring her that all that was left was a carriage drive to Feronia. She remembered nothing of the drive except that it seemed to go on for as long as the train; she sat with her eyes shut and thought of beds, lovely, soft ones that took your shape as you sank into them.

They got out of the carriage and stepped onto some gravel in front of a long, pillared building that was only one story high. Inside it seemed to be sumptuously furnished, and she was led down long, carpeted corridors to a bedroom. There are carpets here anyway, she thought just before she fell asleep. And there aren't any stairs.

She slept long and far on into the morning, and when she woke at last it was only because Suora Imelda was in the room rustling about. She went over to the shutters and threw them back with a clatter, and the sun streamed into the room and Maria blinked. Suora Imelda nodded and smiled to Maria and said something about "*lettera*" which Maria did not understand. She had never managed to pick out where one Italian word finished and another began.

But it was a letter, a letter with an English stamp. It lay on her breakfast tray with a cup of milky coffee and a roll. The writing was round and rather childish and completely unknown to Maria. Besides, who would write to her? Then she thought of Mrs. Clomper. She had never seen her writing; the letter might be from her. And fearing it might, she left it unopened while she drank her coffee. But when she did tear open the envelope and unfolded the sheet inside, tears came into her eyes. It was written from Oxford. It was only a few weeks since she had left Oxford, but she felt as though centuries of time and thousands of miles separated her from it. "Seventeen Bradmore Road, Oxford"—then it was from Harriet. The writing was somehow too neat and careful, Maria had a feeling that there had been several copies before this one was made.

> *Dear Maria,*
>
> *I expect you are rejoicing in blue and cloudless skies. Here there is some sun, but showers in between. However, the trees are breaking into leaf.*
>
> *I am sure you are seeing wonderful things in Italy. You were very fortunate to be asked to go, though I am sorry you did not stay at the Oxford Ladies' College. Mother says that it is a good school, but I expect you are too clever to need to go to school very much. Can you talk Italian now? I found a grammar book among my aunt's books and have tried to learn a little, but I lack perseverance, Mother says.*
>
> *It would be very nice to hear what things you are doing in Italy. I hope you do not mind me writing.*
>
> *With good wishes from your sincere friend,*
> > *Harriet Jessop*

More tears came into Maria's eyes as she read the letter; tears because it was written from Oxford, the one place in the world she wanted to be, and tears because Harriet was so terribly wrong about everything. She thought Maria was having such a wonderful time, but

Maria was not; she hated Italy so much that she would have been glad to see it sunk in the ocean forever.

As soon as she had eaten her breakfast she rummaged in her trunk for her little writing desk, and extracted some paper and a pencil. Then, getting back into bed, she started on the long letter that was to tell Harriet what Italy really was like.

At first she was fairly restrained. "We have been unlucky, Mr. Burghclere says, the weather has been bad; spring is uncertain in northern Italy." But then the memory of those long, dreary days in Venice returned, when she had squelched through the rain, shivered in the cold of the *palazzo*, stared at pictures in the gloom of churches, and she was lashed into furious hatred of it all.

She poured it out, her hand trembled as she covered the sheets of writing paper and became hot and sticky in her anger and excitement. She told Harriet how horrible the food was, how tumbledown and dark and shabby the insides of the houses, how big and cold and cavernous the churches were, and how she never wanted to see another picture or a mosaic as long as she lived. "I would rather go blind," she wrote dramatically. "But I have been ill, and I shall stay ill as long as I am in Italy. Mr. Burghclere wants to show me pictures in Florence, but he cannot while I am in bed."

An Intruder

*M*aria never had time to finish that letter, for Battista came in just then to dress her. She settled her in an armchair near the window, and, smiling brightly at her, moved over a table on which she placed Maria's writing things. And she had barely left the room when there was a knock at the door and Mr. Burghclere came in. Maria went scarlet, and guiltily put her hand over the letter she had just written. Mr. Burghclere also seemed ill at ease. He did not sit down, but held the back of a chair and stared at a point above Maria's head.

"I hope you slept well after the tiring journey."

"Very well, thank you," said Maria, still very confused.

"Perhaps Feronia will suit you better than Venice. You will certainly find it warmer. You might care to sit on the terrace during the day. You can always move back into the shade if it gets too hot."

"That will be very nice," said Maria. There was a long pause.

"I think it would be as well if you did not begin on any studies for some weeks yet," said Mr. Burghclere at last. "If you want to read, there are plenty of books, my own library as well as all Cousin Henry's, which have just arrived from England." He paused, and then added reluctantly, "There are also some other English children fairly near."

"Oh, no," said Maria hastily. "I'm not at all lonely, thank you. I would just like to read."

Mr. Burghclere seemed immensely relieved. "That is easily arranged. You need never be short of books here. You must come and see my library as soon as you feel strong enough. For the moment I shall have my hands full sorting the new books, but no doubt I shall be finished by the time you are ready to take an interest in your studies again."

Maria smiled faintly and wondered whether Mr. Burghclere meant that he expected the arranging of the new books to take a long or a short time. But one thing she was certain of, she was going to drag out her convalescence as long as possible.

"Is that a letter you wish to have posted?" Mr. Burghclere looked at the sheets of paper that Maria was still holding.

She was thrown into a state of miserable and guilty confusion. "I don't know. Well, yes. But it isn't finished yet," she gabbled.

"Giuseppe will be going through the town on his way to take Suora Imelda to the station. You know that she goes back to Venice today? He will post it along with letters of mine."

"I don't want to bother him," said Maria wretchedly.

"I assure you it is no trouble. And no one may be going down for a day or two after this."

Maria could see no way out. She hastily scribbled "With good wishes from Maria Henniker-Hadden" on the last sheet, and thrust the letter into an envelope. She was not sure that she wanted the letter to go at all. She had poured out all her misery more for herself than for anybody else, and it hurt her pride that Harriet of all people should feel sorry for her. But it was too late now, and she had to watch Mr. Burghclere carry off the letter with the air of one doing a kindness.

She worried about it a little, but not for long. She felt in a dreamy, apathetic state, and all she wanted to do was to sit with her hands folded and think about nothing in particular. And the terrace, when Battista took her out later that morning, was just the place for that.

In years to come Maria realized it was an extraordinarily beautiful view. Hills and hills and hills, all purple and blue and gray, lay around her in a vast sweep. It was almost as if she were an eagle flying above them. The hill on which the villa was built was so steep that from the chaise longue where Maria lay she could not see the houses that climbed up the slopes below the terraced garden. All she could see was the low parapet wall at the end of the garden, and then the hills beyond. The chaise longue had been placed on a narrow terrace that ran the whole length of the villa. Down a few steps was the garden, a pretty poor affair if you compared it with an English garden, Maria thought. Still, it did not have the same air of musty desolation as the Venice one. It was a square, laid out with broad gravel paths, tiny box hedges which enclosed flower beds planted out with a few pansies and geraniums, and, down two sides of the garden, tall evergreen hedges (she later discovered they were ilex) which formed shady arbors, and here and there were marble benches rather like tombstones. Then came the parapet, then the hills.

In the mornings the sun was not in the least too hot. She used to lie on the chaise longue on the terrace, letting the warmth soak into her. She felt she would never be tired of that, after those weeks in Venice. Battista would put a table by her, piled with books and writing materials. But she hardly read at first, and nobody ever came to disturb her.

Mr. Burghclere spent all day in the library. It was a

huge and magnificent room on the other side of the villa, overlooking the big, graveled court where their carriage had driven on the day of their arrival. Maria had gone there once, down richly carpeted corridors (the Villa Gondi was a very different place altogether from the Palazzo Malipiero), to see Mr. Burghclere's books, his prints, engravings, coins, and medals (he seemed to collect everything). But he was deeply involved with the arranging of the books from Uncle Hadden's library. He had an Italian secretary, and Giuseppe, but it was all a far more exacting and difficult task than he had realized, he told Maria. He was think-ing of getting a professional cataloguer out from England.

But Maria rejoiced. If he was so busy, he would not have time for her, and all she wanted was to be left alone and not to have to talk to people. She even wished Mr. Burghclere did not feel it was his duty to come and sit with her for half an hour after lunch and in the evening. As for Battista, Maria hardly saw her. She helped Maria dress and undress, she brought her out meals and cool drinks, and there was a bell on Maria's table to call her. What Battista did the rest of the time Maria neither knew nor cared. She suspected she spent some of it with the gardener's boy. She sometimes saw them together in the distance, and once or twice she heard whispering behind the ilex hedges.

When the sun grew stronger in the afternoon, Giuseppe and the gardener's boy would move the chaise longue down off the terrace to the shade of the ilexes, and as Maria walked across to it she could see over the wall a glimpse of the roofs of the houses of the town that lay beyond the hill. She told herself that one day she would lean over the wall and look down. But not just yet, there was plenty of time. And she would lie there all afternoon, staring dreamily at the parapet, at the patterns the ilex leaves made against the sky, and at the long, low façade of the villa.

In some curious Italian architectural fashion, it was only a wing of the villa. She had seen the main block from one of the library windows. It lay at right angles across the graveled court. Mr. Burghclere said that an English family lived there. They had their own garden, however, and Mr. Burghclere never saw anything of them. "They are pleasant enough, but one likes to keep oneself to oneself. We meet only if we happen to come through the main gates at the same time." Maria knew enough of Mr. Burghclere by this time to be certain that such a meeting would be very distasteful to him.

Then one evening, very surprisingly, he brought up the subject of the English family again. Maria and he were sitting together on the terrace. It was the half hour that he habitually spent with her before his dinner, which he now ate alone. The sun had gone down behind the hills, leaving them black silhouettes against the greenish-blue of the sky, and here and there over the horizon drifted flame-colored little clouds, the last relics of the sunset. The swallows dipped and swooped and flashed overhead with sweet, shrill cries. Maria thought that it would really be quite pleasant if only she could be by herself, since neither of them ever knew what to say to the other.

"I met Miss Buldino with two of the girls this afternoon," he said suddenly. "She stopped and asked if there was anything she could do for you, if you would like the girls to come and sit with you sometimes. But I thought you were not strong enough for this yet. Perhaps later. I hope I was right in saying this?"

Maria, who had been feeling quite faint with anxiety at the prospect of having to chatter to strangers, leaned back on her cushions with relief. "Oh, yes," she said weakly. "I would rather not see anybody, please."

"That is what I thought," said Mr. Burghclere with satisfaction.

So Maria found herself safe from disturbance for the immediate future. All that was needed was for her to stay on her chaise longue and behave like an invalid. But in fact she was feeling much better, and as she grew stronger she began to be irked by the limits of the garden, so square, with the villa at one end, the parapet at the other, and the ilex hedges on either side. Even if

Maria had dared walk around it, there would be nothing to see except gravel and pansies and geraniums. She began to hate the garden and the terrace. It was so dry, so dusty, with never a patch of green to refresh it, only the somber, almost black masses of ilex. At home, in Oxford, the cuckoo would be singing, the fields on either side of the Cherwell would be golden with buttercups, the smell of meadow sweet and cow parsley would be in the air, and punts would be slowly drifting down the greeny-brown river. It brought tears to her eyes to think of it.

It was now the beginning of May. The sun was growing hotter, and one particular afternoon Battista suggested that Maria might like to retreat to her bedroom to avoid the heat. But Maria resisted strenuously. She knew that this meant having the shutters closed (Italians seemed to regard open shutters as something unclean), and that it would be evening before Battista appeared again to help her outside. So the chaise longue was moved back as far as possible into the shadows of the ilex. Maria lay there with the sun filtering through the leaves, making patches of shadow and light on her clothes. It was very hot and very still. Nobody was around at all. The servants were all taking a siesta, Mr. Burghclere was in his library, and Maria knew there would not be a sign of life for two or three more hours. She had a volume of poetry beside her, and Scott's

Redgauntlet and Mr. Ruskin's *Stones of Venice.* But she did not want to read any of those; as for *The Stones of Venice* which Mr. Burghclere had pressed upon her, she did not intend to open a page of it. But she was bored, terribly bored, and homesick and restless and miserable. There was not a sound anywhere; even the swallows were no longer swooping and skimming and screaming.

Then Maria heard a faint scritch-scratch below the parapet. She listened idly at first, wondering what it could be, and then she began to be obsessed by the noise. Whatever was it? And what did lie below the parapet anyway? She had never investigated. There was a whole world down there that she knew nothing about. She looked toward the villa; over every window the shutters were drawn, the whole place was asleep. She swung her legs over the chaise longue, looked around her again, and then got up and tiptoed quickly over to the parapet, trying to step as lightly as she could so as to make no crunching sound on the gravel. Eagerly she leaned over the wall.

It was a completely new scene that she had never guessed at. She had vaguely imagined a bare hillside, but a whole town lay there. She was looking down on the browny-red tops of houses, steep little lanes, wash hanging out of windows, and here and there the tower of a church. And at the bottom of the immensely high wall of which the parapet was the top, so high that it seemed to prop up the whole of the hilltop, was an old man in a faded blue shirt and a straw hat hoeing in his vegetable plot. This was the scritch-scratch Maria had heard.

It was, at any rate, a change from the gravel and the hedges of the garden. Giving another quick look around, Maria hoisted herself on the hot stone of the parapet, and, sitting sideways, gazed down at the scene below. But she almost lost her balance and plunged into the faraway vegetable patch in her fright, when a voice suddenly remarked from the ilex bushes: "You're a fraud."

She slithered down on to the gravel again, and stood looking wildly into the shadows of the ilexes, panting and sweating in her fright.

"*I* saw you," said the voice again. "You looked all around to see if anybody was watching, then you got up. But I was there to see."

It was a girl's voice that came from a spot behind the chaise longue. Maria clutched at the parapet and wondered whether to run for the villa.

"Who is it?" she said hoarsely.

"You won't know my name if I tell you," said the voice briskly. "And I can't come through. Oh, perhaps I can."

The noise that the stranger made in trying to do so was tremendous in the stillness of the hot afternoon, and Maria, aghast, watched the villa to see whether people were running out in alarm. At last a girl squeezed through the thick branches and stood there, with disheveled red hair, her hat in her hand, and green stains all over her white dress.

"I'm Cordelia Squerrye," she announced. "Are you Miss Burghclere?"

"I'm Maria Henniker-Hadden," said Maria. "Mr. Burghclere is only my cousin."

"What a pity," remarked the girl. "We always called you Miss Burghclere."

"How do you know me, then?" said Maria faintly.

"My sister Helena succored you with smelling salts during a Channel crossing. You had a stout housekeeperish-looking person with you then. She's not here now, is she?"

Then Maria dimly remembered that family of girls with green coats and green feathers in their hats. A lifetime ago, it seemed. And, of course, Mr. Burghclere had murmured something about their being neighbors, though she had never given it another thought. "Mrs. Clomper went home," she said, still staring at the girl and trying to assess her. "She didn't like Italy."

"How silly. Hadn't you better come out of the sun?"

Maria moved over toward the chaise longue and sat down weakly. She was still staring at her visitor and trying to recover her senses.

"I've been watching you through the hedge for days,

you know," continued the girl. "The hedge is thick, but I made a little window."

Maria pulled her wits together. "What did you say your name was?"

"Cordelia Squerrye. We live in the main part of the villa, you know. Mr. Burghclere's part is only a wing."

Maria was beginning to piece things together. She had seen the main block of the villa from the library. It was a tall, square house of two or more stories. Mr. Burghclere had referred to the English family that lived there; indeed, he had said they suggested calling upon Maria.

Cordelia Squerrye put on her hat again and sat down beside Maria. "What is it like living with a recluse?"

Maria colored, wondering whether this girl meant that she, Maria, was a recluse. "Who do you mean?" she asked in confusion.

"We call Mr. Burghclere the Recluse. He hates talking to anybody. You should see him run away with his eyes turned in the other direction if we do happen to meet. We try to creep up on him unawares so that he *has* to say good morning. Even our governess, Miss Buldino, does that sometimes. So what is it like living with him?"

Maria considered. She had really formed no opinion of Mr. Burghclere at all. He liked books and art and being by himself, that was all she knew. "We don't see very much of each other," she said at last.

Cordelia laughed. "That's just what I told my sisters," she said triumphantly. "I was sure Mr. Burghclere would bury himself in his books and his drawings, no matter who was in the house."

Maria was offended. "In Venice we went out every day and he showed me paintings and churches and mosaics. But then I was ill, and I'm only beginning to get better now," she finished self-righteously.

"Oh, you really have been ill. I'll have to tell Sophy that. She is my second sister, and she had all sorts of romantic ideas about you being some sort of heiress that Mr. Burghclere was keeping hidden away as a prisoner and not allowing to see anybody. She made Miss Buldino ask Mr. Burghclere whether we could come and call on you, and when he said you were not strong enough for visitors, she worked herself into a terrible state, half wanting him to have a prisoner because it was so romantic, and half feeling sorry for you. She reads too many storybooks, that's her trouble, but we have to be indulgent because she is so delicate."

"Well, I was ill," said Maria shortly, enraged that all these people spent their time discussing her affairs. "And I was very glad when Mr. Burghclere said I didn't want callers. You can tell Sophy, whoever she may be, that Mr. Burghclere is very kind to me and that of course I'm not a prisoner. And now, if you don't mind, I think I'll go inside and sleep. I'm supposed to rest in the afternoons."

Over the Wall

And it was inside that Battista found her, some time later, when she came hurrying in search of her. To her agitated questioning Maria merely said that it had been too hot outside. (In spite of herself, she was beginning to speak a little Italian, hardly noticing that she was doing so.) She also said that she wished to stay inside for the rest of the evening. There was one good thing about not being able to speak much Italian, it meant that Battista could not expect proper reasons for her sudden wish to stay indoors.

She was not in truth very clear herself why she was so determined not to see Cordelia Squerrye again. She was, partly, ashamed of having spoken so crossly, but in addition to that, she dreaded the thought of having to talk to people. And as she sat there in her room with the golden-red light from the setting sun stealing through the slats in the shutters, she wondered whether she, too, was becoming a recluse like Mr. Burghclere.

He came to see her that evening. Battista had told him how the signorina had found it too hot outside, and he hoped Maria was not feeling indisposed from the sun. Maria agreed that she had found it a little hot. Then, without meaning to, she found herself asking about the other inhabitants of the Villa Gondi. "You did say that somebody from the villa had asked about me," she added rather shamefacedly.

"That was Miss Buldino. She lives in the other block of the villa, which, by the by, is architecturally quite insignificant, not in the least like this wing, with her charges, four young girls. Their name is Squerrye, they are the daughters of Lord Rivingham, the politician. I believe one of the girls is delicate and has been advised to live abroad, so they spend most of the year here with their governess. Their mother, I gather, is dead. They seem pleasant enough, and Miss Buldino is an amiable lady. We really hardly know each other at all. I dare say I could ask them to call if you wished though." Mr. Burghclere made this last remark very apprehensively, as though he feared Maria might take him at his word.

"Oh, no, thank you," she said hastily. "I would rather be alone."

The next day she refused to allow the chaise longue

to be moved from the terrace into the shadow of the ilex hedge when the afternoon came. She said that she would stay in the drawing room with the glass doors open. No, she did not want the shutters pulled across them. Battista, who seemed to think of the sun as something that must be shut out, like a fog or an east wind, looked astounded, and expostulated. But Maria merely repeated *"Persiane—aperte."* From her peephole in the hedge Cordelia could never see her here, and she could not bear the thought of being imprisoned in a shuttered room for four or five hours. With the glass doors onto the terrace open, she could at least see the hills.

She had not sat in the drawing room before, and, since Mr. Burghclere spent most of his time in the library, it presumably was little used. It was full of rich-looking gilded furniture, statuettes, pieces of porcelain, and at least it gave her new things to look at.

She was feeling pleasantly sleepy after a good lunch (cooking at the Villa Gondi was an enormous improvement on Anna's), and, secure against being spied upon by any of the Squerrye girls, she had just closed her eyes when a faint scrunch of gravel broke the stillness of the afternoon. She sat up in alarm. There, standing in the middle of the hot garden, shading her eyes with her hand and staring around her with the greatest calm, stood Cordelia. Maria fell back among the cushions. Her immediate instinct was to look wildly around the room for a hiding place. But the room was empty of hiding places. All the furniture was pushed back against the walls, leaving a great open space in the middle of the room, unoccupied except by a few flimsy gilded armchairs. All she could do was lie down behind her chaise longue, and she hurled herself off and crawled on her hands and knees around to the back. There, with her heart thudding wildly, she crouched and listened.

Footsteps advanced slowly over the gravel. Then, to her horror, Maria saw underneath the chaise longue a shadow stretching from the door over the carpet. The shadow moved, and a voice said over her head: "Whatever are you doing there?"

Maria's fright, her resentment that she had been caught in such a ridiculous position, made her furiously angry. She sat up on her heels and stared at Cordelia Squerrye, who was kneeling on the chaise longue and looking down at her. "Why have you come in here? I want to go to sleep!"

"Oh, you're all right, then," remarked Cordelia coolly. "I was afraid you had had a fit or a faint, and I didn't know whether to ring for a servant or send for Miss Buldino."

"Why have you come here?" repeated Maria angrily. She pulled herself up from the floor and gripped the back of the sofa with a trembling hand.

"Sophy wants to see you. She couldn't sleep all night

for wanting to. Mr. Burghclere doesn't wish us to call upon you in the usual way, so I thought I had better take matters into my own hands."

Maria was outraged. "Of course I can't come. I'm still supposed to be ill. I lie here all day."

"*Supposed* is the right word. You and I know you don't lie there all day."

"It was only just that one day that I got up," said Maria hotly. "I heard a noise and wanted to see what it was. It is very boring in the garden."

Cordelia was completely unruffled. "If you are bored by your garden, it is all the more reason why you should come and see ours. And show Sophy that you are not a prisoner wasting away. You have hardly farther to walk than you did yesterday. But you had better hurry, because they will be wondering where I am."

Cordelia was the most masterful person Maria had ever met. It was like a steam engine bearing down upon her, and she felt quite helpless. Miserably, she trailed out into the heat behind Cordelia, who was striding purposefully down the steps from the terrace. Maria, however, kept peering furtively back at the house as she went. At the ilex hedge Cordelia stopped.

"Shall I go through first? Then I can make the hole bigger."

But Maria remembered the state in which Cordelia had emerged yesterday. However could she explain

tears and stains all over her dress to Battista, who supposed Maria had been sitting in the drawing room all
afternoon? "I'm not going through," she said sulkily.
"Look what happened to your dress yesterday."

"Then do you want to go right through your house
and out by the front door?"

"No, of course I don't," said Maria angrily. "I don't
want to come at all."

Cordelia took no notice whatever. "Then if you
don't want to go through the hedge or through the front
door, you'll have to walk down the wall." She went to
the parapet. "It's possible."

The parapet, in fact, continued beyond the ilex
hedge, and as Cordelia said, it was, in theory, possible
to clamber up, squeeze a few steps past the hedge, and
jump down in the garden on the other side. But you
would have to have the nerve of a mountain goat
because of the terrifying drop far, far down to the vegetable patch where Maria had seen the old man hoeing.
She peeped over again and then drew back in horror.

"Yes, I know it's high up," said Cordelia briskly. "But
the parapet is broad and it probably *is* a much better way
than through the hedge. I'll go first. It's only a few
steps."

She climbed up, and, holding on to the ilexes, disappeared from sight. Maria watched in fascinated horror,
but she did not attempt to escape.

"Come on, it's much easier than it looks," called Cordelia from the other side of the hedge. "Face the bushes and hold on to them and take three steps and you're there."

This was all very well, but first she had to climb up, with nothing to conceal the precipitous drop below. Maria, as she crouched on top of the parapet, not daring to straighten her knees, stared giddily down, feeling that the stony earth far, far below was pulling her, that inevitably she must crash down to it.

"Come on," said Cordelia impatiently. "Do you want to be seen from the house?"

Fear made Maria do what she could not otherwise have achieved. She stood up, turned, clutched at the ilex twigs, and shuffled sideways. Just ahead of her a muslin-covered arm stretched up. She almost hurled herself at it, and then fell off the parapet into the garden on the other side of the hedge.

"You'd better let me brush you a little." Cordelia banged at Maria's dress with an ungentle hand. "I think you had better not say anything to Miss Buldino about the way we came. She worries so much about us. Come on."

The Squerryes' garden was much the same as Mr. Burghclere's. There were gravel paths and little box hedges, and flower beds with geraniums and pansies. But it was bigger, and the parapet was separated from

the garden by another thick hedge, so that one could walk along the gravel path in front of it and admire the view over the wall without being seen from the house. As Maria followed Cordelia she could hear a murmur of voices from a downstairs room whose glass doors were ajar.

"They're in here." Cordelia stepped back to allow Maria to go in. The room was darkened by shutters and venetian blinds, but Maria was conscious of a number of people sitting around a table and staring at her. "I have brought Miss Henniker-Hadden to call upon you, since Mr. Burghclere dislikes the idea of us calling upon him," announced Cordelia. "Miss Henniker-Hadden, these are my sisters Helena, Sophia, and Jane. And Miss Buldino, of course."

There was a startled murmuring, and the sound of chairs scraping upon marble floors as the girls rose to their feet. Maria's eyes had become accustomed to the dimmer light, and she recognized them as the girls she had noticed with a momentary interest on board the Channel steamer. There was a tall girl of fifteen or sixteen, her fair hair tied back with a big black bow. It was she who had been so ready with eau de cologne and smelling salts. Then there were two younger girls, one tall with thin cheeks and large eyes, and the other a mere child of seven or eight, round and rosy. The lady who was sitting with them came forward, the middle-aged person with pince-nez on a golden chain who had been looking so unwell when Maria had seen her before.

"But, Cordelia dear, this is very unexpected. Surely you did not actually presume to call upon Mr. Burghclere after he had so expressly said that the little girl was not ready for callers."

Then she turned anxiously to Maria. "How do you do, my dear, I'm the governess. I hope we see you well."

"Mr. Burghclere did not raise any objection this time," said Cordelia with a coolness that astounded Maria. She had never thought that somebody of her own age could be so poised, so calm, and so much in command of the situation.

"But to call upon the villa by yourself, dear," fluttered Miss Buldino. "That, surely . . . Jane, my love, fetch a chair for Miss Henniker-Hadden. If she has been unwell, I expect she finds this heat trying."

The round, rosy child fetched a chair for Maria, keeping her head turned over her shoulder to stare as she went. Then everybody settled down in a circle of chairs to look at Maria. Or that was how it felt.

"Sophy was fretting to see Mr. Burghclere's prisoner," Cordelia went on calmly. "And you know what restless nights do for her. Mr. Burghclere had made it quite plain that he does not care for visitors, but he doesn't seem to mind what Miss Henniker-Hadden does while he is in the library."

"Well, as long as he hasn't taken it amiss, dear," said Miss Buldino doubtfully, "and the little girl hasn't done herself any harm by coming out in the heat. Of course we are all delighted to see her."

"I hope *you* are specially delighted, Sophy," remarked Cordelia. "But she doesn't look like anybody's prisoner, does she? Or wasting away?"

But the thin-faced Sophia could only stare and giggle while her cheeks grew more and more flushed.

"Sophy," said the oldest girl reprovingly. "You will bring on a coughing attack if you don't take care."

"Besides, you are too old to giggle like that," added the governess mildly. "Miss Henniker-Hadden will think you very ill bred. I hope Mr. Burghclere has no objection to you coming over here, dear," she said to Maria. "I know he is a gentleman who likes solitude. . . ."

Maria had opened her mouth to tell Miss Buldino that Mr. Burghclere knew nothing whatever of her movements, that nobody in the villa did, that Cordelia had carried her off against her will, and that she was very angry about it all. But Cordelia intervened.

"I am sure Mr. Burghclere is very pleased to have his solitude increased," she said coolly.

The younger girls tittered, and even Miss Buldino smiled a little. "Yes, he is a gentleman who prefers to be by himself, but Cordelia, my love, I am not sure that you should speak like that. Remember this little girl is Mr. Burghclere's niece."

"Cousin," Maria corrected her, extremely irritated by Cordelia's manner. "Third cousin once removed."

The younger girls tittered again. Helena looked at them reprovingly and started to make conversation.

"It is so nice that you have called, Miss Henniker-Hadden. We have tried to call ourselves, but Mr. Burghclere did not seem to wish it, so we have not pressed the matter. I hope you soon recovered after the Channel crossing."

"I didn't mind that so much," said Maria. "It was Venice that was so horrible, so wet and so cold, and the palace was horrid and I was so ill."

"Yes, I believe Venice can be very rainy in the spring," said Helena with the air of a much-traveled person. "But I am sure you will like it here."

"I don't know," said Maria wearily. "I haven't liked it very much so far, though the sun is nice, of course."

Miss Buldino was tactful. "You'll get used to it, dear. It probably does seem rather strange at first. We spend eight months of the year here, and though we were glad to see England again last June, we were very glad to be back at the Villa Gondi in October. Now I think I hear them bringing in the tea. I hope we can persuade you to stay and have it with us."

Maria was doubtful; supposing somebody came and

found her sofa empty? She had been mad to agree to go with Cordelia in the first place, and it would be the veriest lunacy to stay and drink tea with these people just as though she were paying an ordinary visit. But when a maid brought in the tray of tea things a few minutes later, she found herself agreeing to stay. The girls were all so pressing, and the tea looked so English and so delicious. The sewing bags were cleared away, a white cloth laid over the table, and they all drew up their chairs and settled down to eat thin bread and butter and jam and Madeira cake, and drink tea poured from a comfortable brown pot.

Maria had not felt so happy and at ease for months. She forgot that she liked to be alone, that she disliked the company of other girls, and she settled down to chatter and to enjoy herself. She learned that Sophia had a bad cough and had been ordered to spend most of the year in Italy, that when Maria had seen them in March they had been back to take Sophia to see a London doctor. Sophia liked storybooks better than anything else in the world, but Jane liked dolls and her canary bird, Twitty, whose cage hung in the window. Helena was seventeen next year and would be coming out. She gave the impression of never doing anything for her own pleasure but devoting herself to her younger sisters.

Cordelia said little. She seemed to be sitting back

smugly, having achieved what she had set out to do. But Maria, now full of tea and well-being, had really quite forgotten the steps Cordelia had taken to bring her here. Indeed, she had forgotten that she was not paying a perfectly orthodox visit.

Down the Steps

When Maria left, the girls were flattering in their pleas that she should come again. Even the august Helena hoped to see her soon, and Miss Buldino told her that it had made a very pleasant interlude, especially for the younger sisters, who otherwise never saw other English children. Cordelia said that she would accompany Maria home. She scoffed at Miss Buldino's suggestion that she should take a maid, and shooed away Jane, who wanted to come too. (Sophia, it seemed, was not allowed out in the heat of the afternoon.)

"We can't have anybody with us if you're to go back by the wall," she remarked to Maria as she led her away through the garden.

"I don't have to go back along it again!" said Maria in horror.

"Do you want to make a state entry in through your front door, then, and ring the bell too?"

Of course that was out of the question, and Maria was by this time so eager to be back that in the end she scrambled along the parapet without giving much thought to the terrifying drop below. She almost fell into the garden and ran back to the house, wondering whether she would find anxious servants ransacking the rooms for her.

But there was her sofa, exactly as she had left it, the cushions tumbled on the floor because of her wild attempts to elude Cordelia. And the house was still and lifeless, nobody was calling her name. As she picked up her cushions and sank down among them, she was conscious of feeling flat and low and lonely after the excitement of the last hour.

When Mr. Burghclere came to sit with her later on, he noticed two things with concern, the fact that she had not read a single page of *The Stones of Venice*, and that Maria's supper tray was being carried from the room largely uneaten. (For had she not just consumed large quantities of bread and raspberry jam and Madeira cake?) He looked disturbed.

"I had been going to suggest that you might care for a drive one morning. But I am not sure that you are up to it. What do you think yourself?"

"I am quite happy here," said Maria faintly.

Mr. Burghclere looked even more concerned. "It seems to me that you are not making as much progress as might be expected. I wonder if I ought to seek more medical advice?"

Maria was thrown into a great state of alarm. "Oh, no, I'm sure I'm getting better. It's just that I like lying here."

Mr. Burghclere looked unconvinced. "Well, we shall have to see how things go on."

Why has one got to be either better or worse? Maria thought gloomily. Why don't people allow you to go on being just the same? Clearly it was going to be far more complicated than she thought to draw out this convalescence of hers indefinitely. And there were increased complications the following morning.

There was a letter from Harriet, which made Maria remember with an uncomfortable jolt the wretched letter she had herself written the day after she had arrived at the Villa Gondi, which she had never really intended should be posted.

> *Dear Maria,*
>
> *I am sorry that Italy is as horrible as you say. Do you know that piece of poetry "Oh to be in England now that April's here"? We had to learn it for our English lesson and it made me feel very sad when I thought of you. (Of course I know it's May now.)*

*Everything looks very pretty in Oxford. There
seem to be flowers on all the trees in all the gardens
and some of the classes (not ours, though) have
even had lessons in the school garden. Papa took me
in a boat up the river to Godstow on Saturday. It
would have been so nice if you were with us.*

Your affectionate friend and well-wisher,

Harriet Jessop

P. S. *Papa thought I could put "affectionate." I hope
you do not mind?*

But this was not all, there was a letter from Dr. Jessop
to Mr. Burghclere, inquiring how Maria was. Mr.
Burghclere came to the terrace where Maria was sitting,
holding this in his hand. He seemed to scrutinize her
thoughtfully, and Maria shrank back against her cushions with a guilty blush. How rude and ungrateful Mr.
Burghclere must think her, pouring out complaints
behind his back to somebody she hardly knew!

"I'm very sorry," she said hysterically. "I was feeling
very tired that day and I said silly things. I didn't really
mean them."

Mr. Burghclere shook his head. "I am not sure that
Italy is agreeing with you. Perhaps it is the climate you
find trying, as Dr. Jessop says. It might be better if you
went back to England for a while."

Though Maria might sigh for Oxford, going back

to England she felt certain could mean only one thing, going back to school. Her voice became more hysterical.

"Oh, no, please not. I don't want to go back to England. I'll do anything you say. I will get better, really I will, and I'll start lessons again," she finished wildly, trying to think of all the things that might persuade Mr. Burghclere to keep her from England and school.

But he did not seem at all satisfied. "My dear Maria, you are in no way fit to begin lessons again." And he stalked away with Dr. Jessop's letter in his hand.

All day long Maria brooded, tossing the matter over in her mind, wondering what to do. It seemed it was too late now to decide to emerge from her convalescence, to offer to go for drives, to look at pictures in Florence. Mr. Burghclere believed that she really was still ill; she had acted her part too well. She could not settle down to read, nor lie back and enjoy the sun, and after lunch it was the same; she sat in the shadow of the drawing room, tormented with worry. She was sorry now that she had kept up her sofa-reclining state so long. Sight-seeing, after all, was not such a horror as school in England. Her fear of it lay in the idea that one picture-gazing trip would lead to another and then another, until she was swept up into the same whirl of churches and pictures and museums as she had had inflicted upon her in Venice. It was like little Henry Fairchild in *The Fairchild Family*, who refused to learn an easy Latin lesson because he realized that it could only lead to more difficult ones.

Marie was so intent upon her troubles that she was quite unaware of anybody coming up the garden toward the house, and she was biting a fingernail in her anguish when Cordelia appeared on the terrace. Maria gave a jump and bit off a piece of her nail. Cordelia's eyes fell on her, and she strolled in.

"Didn't you hear me calling you from the hedge? I must say I don't like having to come up the garden like this. I suppose they are all having their siesta here, but there always might be someone to see me. Why can't you sit in the garden like you used to?"

"I suppose you want me to come into your garden again," said Maria snappily.

"I want you to help me in a private scheme of mine."

"Well, I'm not going to crawl along that parapet again."

"I'm afraid you will have to. But you need not see my sisters again."

"I liked your sisters." Maria hoped to convey by this that she liked Helena, Sophia, and Jane a great deal better than their sister.

"Yes, they seem to have liked you. You can see them another day, perhaps. What I want to do today is to look at Feronia."

Maria stared. "How do you mean?"

"This town, here. I've never seen it properly, and I

am sure you haven't. Of course we go out for drives with Miss Buldino, and we've been to Florence, but I want just to poke about for myself and see the people."

"You don't mean by yourself?" Maria could not believe she had understood properly.

"Of course I can't go by myself," said Cordelia impatiently. "You're going to come with me."

"Me?" said Maria faintly. Then she tried to assert herself. "Of course I can't. Nor can you either."

"Give me one good reason why we can't. Only hurry, we haven't got so very much time."

The whole notion was so preposterous that Maria could not think of cut and dried reasons. "We wouldn't be allowed to. How can we without somebody to go with us? Among all those Italians too!" she gabbled at last.

"The Italians are charming," said Cordelia decisively. "Very friendly and polite. Nobody has told me I shouldn't go. Have they told you? And lastly, there is nobody to go with me, they are all sleeping, and I expect it is the same here. If you have no other objections to offer, we had better start."

Once again Maria, in spite of all her longing to resist, found herself following Cordelia. Passively she went out into the garden, clambered along the parapet again behind Cordelia, and jumped into the garden on the other side of the hedge.

"There's a door and some steps along here,"

announced Cordelia. "I thought the door was locked, but it was just very stiff and rusty and I've gotten it open."

She led the way down the path that ran by the side of the parapet. There was a high wall at the far end, and there was a door that Cordelia had spoken about. It looked as though it had not been opened this century, its paint had worn down to the bare wood, its handle was eaten with rust. But Cordelia, after much tugging and muttering, managed to open it. Below lay a terrifying flight of steps stretching steeply down the precipitous hill that the villa was built on. There seemed to be hundreds and hundreds of them, going down to a little patch of grass at the bottom. Maria drew back in consternation.

"Yes, I know, it is steep," said Cordelia. "We'll have to allow plenty of time coming back. But think how nice it will be running down." And she started plunging ahead.

Maria could not feel the same. The sun was hot and the steps made the muscles of her legs ache fiercely. From time to time on the descent she glanced back at the door high above them, tiny in the distance, looking completely unattainable now. She reached the grass patch sometime after Cordelia, and sat weakly down on the bottom step. Cordelia pointed to a dusty, stony track some yards away.

"That's the road that goes down into the town. It's

the one we drive up and down on our way from the villa."

When Maria had eased her aching legs, they sauntered on down the little road. The dust and stones turned into cobbles before very long and the road wound between houses. Maria, in spite of herself, began to enjoy it. This was the sort of lingering expedition she had longed for all the time she was in Venice. She found she could look in through the street-level windows of the houses. Overhead, wash hung on lines stretched from house to house, birds twittered in cages hung at upper windows. Sometimes in a damp-smelling cavern that opened on to the street she would catch a glimpse of men mending chairs or making shoes or beating out metal, and there was nobody to hurry her or to care how much she stared, certainly not Cordelia. The road wound down and down between the houses. There were few people around; just occasionally they met a black-pinafored child, barefooted, clutching a loaf or a jug, who stopped to stare.

Maria suddenly felt happy. "It would have been all right in Venice if it had been like this. But it was always churches and mosaics and pictures. I don't want to see another picture again in my life."

"How foolish you are," remarked Cordelia loftily. "Florence is full of the most wonderful things. The Botticellis in the Uffizi! The pity of it was that Miss Buldino would hurry us on so. Perhaps Mr. Burghclere would agree to take me with you to Florence one day. I'm sure he understands about looking at pictures."

Maria stopped dead. "I'm never going to look at another picture," she said violently as memories of those painful sightseeing expeditions in Venice swept over her again. "Never. I'm never going to get well enough to go out with Mr. Burghclere again. If I have to look at a picture, I think I will be sick."

Cordelia looked at her angry face with interest. "So that's why you lie on the sofa all the time. I did wonder. I thought it was just because you liked being an invalid. It's more like a storybook than even Sophy imagined. Though I am afraid that Miss Buldino would call it all rather deceitful."

Maria flushed. "I don't think it's deceitful," she began. "If you knew how miserable I was in Venice—"

Cordelia stopped her. "Oh, don't worry, I don't propose to tell anybody about your extraordinary behavior."

They went on down the street, and suddenly emerged out of the shadows into the blaze and heat of an open square. There were some picturesque old buildings and a church, a fountain in the middle, a great deal of sun, and no people at all. Cordelia blinked and stared at the fountain, where water ran in trickles out of the mouths of a number of grotesque monsters.

"Look at those pigeons drinking. They make me feel so thirsty." She pointed at the pigeons who perched on the heads of the monsters, twisting their necks and holding open their beaks to catch the water that trickled from the mouths. "The trouble is that I won't get any tea today, because they all think at the villa that I'm drinking tea with you."

Maria was scandalized. "It's you who's deceitful, not me."

Cordelia remained tranquil. "There's no deceit in it. I certainly didn't *tell* them that I was having tea with you. I merely said that I was going to visit you, and they assumed Mr. Burghclere must have asked me to tea."

"Without asking any questions or anything?" Maria remembered how Mrs. Clomper had wanted particulars of every movement of hers, and had even escorted her down the road when she visited the Smith boys in Canterbury Lane.

"Oh, they leave me pretty much to myself. They're so busy with Sophy, poor little thing. They did say that it was rather curious that Mr. Burghclere hadn't sent over a note, but then, he is so very odd that they realized he would never think of such things. Now, the point is I am hungry and thirsty. I still have one lira left from when we bought birthday presents for Papa in Florence. Shall we go to that café and order some lemonade?"

There seemed to be no limit to Cordelia's preposter-ous audacity. With feeble expostulations, to which Cordelia paid not the slightest attention, Maria crossed the square after her companion. There were two cafés here, one had a striped awning over the pavement, the other orange umbrellas. Cordelia inspected both criti-cally, and then sat down at a table under the striped awning. There was a sleepy-looking waiter lounging against a doorpost, and Cordelia beckoned him over imperiously.

"*Buona sera, signor. Due limonate, per favore,*" she said with great aplomb, and without the slightest embarrassment.

The waiter showed no surprise at receiving orders from such a young customer. He repeated, "*Due limonate. Subito, signorina,*" and disappeared into the shop.

"Do you often do this?" said Maria, amazed.

"Of course not. When would I get the chance?"

"But the waiter didn't think it was at all strange," said Maria incredulously.

"Italians are very polite. Besides, the thing is to be bold. Always walk into a place as if it is your own, hold your head up, and you can take even the Crown Jewels. That's what my godfather says."

"It doesn't sound like most godfathers." Maria thought of Great-Uncle Matthew, now long-ago dead.

As far as she could remember, he never said anything to her except that he hoped she was a good girl and knew her catechism.

"Oh, he isn't. He's a bachelor for one thing. I much prefer bachelors, don't you?"

"I don't know," said Maria, startled. "Uncle Hadden was a bachelor, so is Mr. Burghclere. But I don't think either would tell me about taking the Crown Jewels."

"How literal you are," said Cordelia impatiently. "You are nearly as bad as Jane."

The waiter came back with their lemonade. It was fizzy, in a tall glass, and Maria drank it gratefully, and then wondered miserably whether it would give her fever. Mrs. Clomper certainly would not have allowed her to drink Italian lemonade at a wayside café. For a moment or two she convinced herself that she could feel the fever coming on now, then she forgot about it because there were far more immediate worries. It might have been pleasant sitting here drowsily in the shade of the awning, looking at the fountain in the middle of the square, where the pigeons preened and strutted, if this had been a properly conducted and arranged visit.

But the enormity of the thing they were doing now fully dawned on Maria. They had stolen away from their homes, nobody knew where they were, nobody could rescue them if they got into difficulties. They were in completely alien territory, and even if they could find their way back, even if Maria's legs, which now felt limp and aching, could carry her so far, it would still be an hour or more before they were back where they belonged. Maria swallowed the last of her lemonade in a gulp and leaned forward and grasped the edge of the table in her anxiety. Cordelia sighed.

"Oh, dear, you're in a fidget already." She did not hurry, however. Maria watched her, in an agony of mind that hardly allowed her to sit still, sipping her lemonade delicately and gazing casually around her. Then at last she beckoned the waiter, paid him, frowned over the change, put down a couple of small coins on the table, and stood up. Maria leapt up with such force that she knocked over her chair and it fell clattering on to the pavement. She was too agitated to care, however.

"Are we going back now?"

"In a moment. I want to buy some doughnuts. There's a little shop over there where they make them while you watch. We always pass it when we go out for a drive."

Cordelia strolled across the square. She paused to look at the fountain, to scrutinize the game of hop-scotch that barefooted urchins were playing on the broad steps of the church, and then took an infinitely long time to find the doughnut maker. They discovered it at last, a tiny slit of a shop, and there Maria had to stand by while the man dropped spoonfuls of soft dough into the bubbling fat, took them out, and rolled them in sugar. Across the square a clock struck, and Maria jumped.

"Four o'clock," announced Cordelia. "We've hardly been out an hour yet, and they won't be expecting me home until half past five at the earliest. Shall we explore some of these side streets?"

"No!" squeaked Maria. "We've got to get home. Now."

Cordelia took the parcel of doughnuts—the fat was already beginning to stain the paper—and nodded to the doughnut maker. "It's no pleasure being out with somebody who is fidgeting all the time, so I suppose we'll have to go. But you know perfectly well that in your establishment nobody will come to their senses until six o'clock. They sleep all afternoon—your Battista told our maid so. Come on, then. We'll eat the doughnuts when we get to the steps, to encourage us."

Maria tried not to walk fast as they trudged up the cobbles of the little street that led out of the town. She did not want to irritate Cordelia by her anxiety to be home. In any case, long before the cobbles turned to dusty white road, she was weary and thinking wistfully of the cushions of the chaise longue. They were at last within sight of the cliff on which the villa was built, and the cool tranquility of the Villa Gondi no longer seemed so impossibly unattainable as it had seemed in the town, when they heard a clop of hooves and the sound of carriage wheels coming up the street toward them. Cordelia looked interested.

"Now, I wonder who that could be. The only place this road goes to is the Villa Gondi, and whoever's behind us must be going there too. Is Mr. Burghclere expecting anybody, do you know?"

Maria did not know, but she felt apprehensive. She scuttled off the road into the coarse grass that led to the foot of the steps, and looked around wildly for somewhere to conceal herself.

"Sit on the steps," said Cordelia. "They won't look, and I want to see who it is."

There was certainly nowhere else to go, so Maria did as she was told, trying to cower in the shadow of the walls. The sound of the horses came nearer, going slowly because of the heat and the hill, and a moment later the equipage came into sight, a smart open carriage with two sleek bays and a liveried coachman. The passenger was a white-bearded man with a glossy silk hat. Cordelia shaded her eyes to look.

"I know who that is," she said suddenly. "It's Dr. Manfrini. He came to see Sophy once. But he's not coming to see her today, nor any of us. Is he coming to see Mr. Burghclere, do you think? He must be, that's Mr. Burghclere's carriage, I recognize the coachman."

Then Maria remembered everything all at once, Mr.

Burghclere's anxiety, his talk of calling in medical advice, the letter Dr. Jessop had written to him. She jumped to her feet and stared wildly at Cordelia. "He's coming to see me!"

"Well," said Cordelia calmly. "There's one thing. He'll take much longer to get there than we will. You've no idea what a long way that road goes around. We've only got to go up the steps."

14

An Invalid Again

*T*he climb back up those steps was nightmarish beyond belief. It would have been bad enough anyway, but Maria was tired, there was an enormous number of them, and the sun was very hot. And to have to take them at a gallop in the heat of the afternoon when you have been lying for weeks on an invalid's sofa! When at last she reached the top, Maria reeled against the door post. Her ears were singing, there was a red mist in front of her eyes, and her shoulders, her side, and her legs felt as though they were being stabbed by hot knives. She did not wait to see what had happened to Cordelia. She pushed the gate open, scuttled through the garden, and somehow dragged herself over the parapet onto the other side.

She had thought that the garden might be full of people searching for her. But the gravel walks and the terrace were as still and as deserted as when she had left them, and the windows of the villa all firmly shuttered against the sun. She ran across the gravel, feebly now, staggered up the low step into the drawing room and flung herself onto the chaise longue. She was limp with exhaustion and emotion. Her head was aching violently, and she was hot and sticky. She mopped her face with a pocket handkerchief, but her hands felt almost too weak to move.

In the distance a bell jangled. Maria stiffened. It must be the doctor! She strained her ears. There were distant footsteps, the murmur of voices. Some minutes passed, during which Maria tried to compose herself, to dry her face, which prickled with sweat and heat, and to stop her hands from trembling. Then voices and footsteps came near. With a strained and anxious expression Maria waited.

Mr. Burghclere was speaking Italian when he opened the door. Maria turned her head and saw him standing there, holding the handle. Beside him and already looking in her direction was the white-bearded doctor.

"Dr. Manfrini has very kindly come out from Florence to see you, Maria. Just in case there is some little thing wrong that is preventing your complete recovery." Then Mr. Burghclere shut the door and went away.

Maria watched Dr. Manfrini like a mesmerized rabbit. Had he seen her quarter of an hour before? Was he going to accuse her of feigning to be ill, of wildly improper behavior? He came forward with a pleasant smile, rubbing his hands together; he took a small gilt chair and placed it squarely by the side of the chaise longue. Then he picked up Maria's wrist and pulled out a gold watch from his waistcoat pocket. Maria relaxed with an audible sigh of relief. He was not going to ask any questions about what she had been doing. He must think she really was an invalid.

In fact, as she grasped within a minute or so, Dr. Manfrini and she had no language in common, so it would have been difficult for him to question her about anything. Instead, he confined himself to scrutinizing her throat and sounding her chest. Maria at first felt light-headed with relief, but then she began to wonder a little uneasily about what sort of report he would make to Mr. Burghclere. Would he say that she was perfectly well and fit, able to resume lessons and sightseeing? She stared at him, wondering what he was thinking. He was certainly making a very careful investigation.

In the end she grew very tired of the investigation, of Dr. Manfrini's plump, white, well-manicured hands, of the scent of eau de cologne that clung to him. He left her at last, with a bow and a smile. But even then she was not left alone. Battista hurried in with an agitated expression and told her that the doctor wished her to go to her own room and retire to bed. Battista was followed by Mr. Burghclere, whose expression was grave. He told her that Dr. Manfrini had not found her as well as he thought she should be, and that he wished her to stay in her room for the next few days.

At first Maria was too exhausted by the events of the afternoon to care about anything. She gratefully drank the cool drinks Battista brought her, fell into bed, and slept for about fourteen hours without stirring. But the next day, when she found she was not allowed to leave her bed, she was very cast down. By the second day she was in despair. In fact, she wept. There seemed no way out of it now. She had acted so well that everybody was convinced she was ill. But Dr. Manfrini ought to have seen through it. If he thought she was really ill, what did he think was wrong? She began to wonder uneasily whether she might have something seriously wrong with her, whether she was dying in a foreign country. More than anything, she wanted comfort, sympathy, somebody to confide in. But there was nobody, there never had been anybody who was at all interested in what she thought and felt.

Then she remembered Harriet. Harriet cared, and though Maria felt ill at ease when she was with her, she could be eloquent in a letter. So she demanded pencil and paper and poured it all out.

I do not know whether Italy is horrid or not. For I no longer see it. Formerly I lay outside in the garden here, but now even that is forbidden to me. I keep to my room and lie in bed. I do not know what is wrong with me, for there is no one here who speaks English except Mr. Burghclere, and I see little of him. I believe he spends most of his time in his library, arranging Uncle Hadden's books. When he sits with me we have little to talk about. Sometime perhaps I will do reading with him again, but I do not think this will be very soon.

I do not like Italian doctors, they are scented and wear rings.

Maria hesitated here, then with a sudden impulse of warmth she wrote:

Write to me soon, you are the only friend I have.
Your affectionate friend,
Maria Henniker-Hadden

This letter and the feeling that Harriet was her only friend made her spirits so low that she was very moist about the eyes when Mr. Burghclere came to pay his morning visit. He made his usual inquiries about her health, there were the usual long pauses and silences, and then he suddenly said, "I think you need company. I shall avail myself of Miss Buldino's offer and ask her to

call with the girls. Yes, I will do that," he concluded
with the air of one making up his mind to a particularly
unpleasant duty.

And so it came about that that afternoon Maria had
two visitors, Helena and Cordelia. Helena, of course,
was sedate and dignified. But this time Cordelia was
too. She behaved so prettily and demurely that she
might have been a younger version of Helena.

"Miss Buldino feels that four of us is too many," she
said charmingly to Maria. "Besides, Sophy is not really
supposed to go out while the sun is hot. So we have
brought over these silhouettes to amuse you."

The three girls sat and turned over the cut-out paper
pictures that Miss Buldino had snipped. They were
undeniably very clever, little profiles of the girls, groups
of people, animals, but it was rather wearying to think
of the right comments to make.

"It's dear Miss Buldino's one great talent," said Cordelia with a flash of her own manner. "That and making
wreaths of flowers for us to wear on our birthdays. They
both belong to a past age, like Miss Buldino herself. She
made us all do samplers, can you imagine it?"

"Cordelia!" said Helena in her reproving elder-sister
way. "You give Miss Henniker-Hadden quite the wrong
impression of Miss Buldino. She is the dearest person,
more like a mother to us than anything else."

"Of course she is, but I don't see what that has to do

with it. The trouble with you, Helena, is that you don't argue properly."

"I hope I do not argue at all. It is not at all the sort of thing I care to do. Nor should you, Cordelia."

Cordelia sighed, and let the silhouettes on her lap slide onto the floor. Then she stood up and wandered over to the window. She peered out through the slats of the shutters.

"Do you know, Helena, the view from here really is very beautiful. You ought to sketch it, I am sure Mr. Burghclere would allow you to."

Helena excused herself to Maria and went to stand by the window. "It certainly is very impressive," she murmured, "the garden, then the parapet, then the hills beyond. Our view from the garden is spoiled by the hedge in front of the parapet."

"Why don't you go out and see," urged Cordelia. "I'm sure you could, aren't you, Maria?"

"Of course she can if she wants to." Maria rather resented the way Cordelia arranged everybody's activities.

"I think you ought to go, Helena. A sketch of the view would make a splendid late birthday present for Papa. Or a Christmas present if you like. You ought to do it before we go back to England. I expect I can find the way out for you." And she had gone, ushering Helena before her.

A minute or two later Cordelia was back alone. "I hope it takes her a long time. Are you really ill?"

"I don't know," said Maria dolefully. "That Dr. Manfrini seems to think I am, I don't know why. I *think* I feel all right," she added doubtfully.

"We heard that you had a dangerous fever and that everybody was fearfully alarmed," said Cordelia with relish.

Maria herself was alarmed. "I didn't know I had that. Who says so?"

"Your maid, Battista, told one of our maids, and she told me. She said Mr. Burghclere sent Giuseppe to fetch Dr. Manfrini from Florence because he thought you weren't well, but when Dr. Manfrini came he found you in a raging fever. If he'd seen you running up the steps! I'm not surprised you looked feverish afterward, I couldn't do it at that speed, especially with all that fizzy lemonade inside me. Which reminds me, you never had the doughnuts. I was left with four of them, I couldn't think what to do with them, so I had to eat them all—I never want to see another doughnut. Anyway, they were not at all good."

Maria disregarded all this chatter about doughnuts. "You don't think I'm ill, then?" she demanded feverishly.

"I wouldn't say you were, no. You're certainly not like Sophy, hectically excited and weak. And look how you rushed up those steps! It was a pity we had such a short time in the town. Another time we shall have to start earlier."

The idea that Cordelia intended to repeat that terrible expedition made Maria feel quite sick. The memory of the afternoon three days ago was so painful that she dared not allow herself to dwell on it. They had escaped detection by a matter of minutes, and only because she had made Cordelia drink up her lemonade quickly—and here was Cordelia calmly talking as though the affair were to be an everyday occurrence.

"I can't go out of this room until Dr. Manfrini says I may," she said weakly.

"I am not proposing that you should," said Cordelia coldly. "I know all about Dr. Manfrini's methods. Let me see, he has told you that you must take an afternoon sleep, and read no storybooks, for storybooks enervate the female brain. But even Dr. Manfrini allows his patients to rise from their beds after a time, and the fact that you are supposed to be shut up in your room sleeping in the afternoons will make it easier for you to slip off without anybody knowing."

When Helena came in from the garden, Maria was lying back on her pillows limply, her mind entirely preoccupied with the thought of Cordelia's expeditions. She felt she could neither eat nor sleep while these threatened her. Conversation between the two girls had stopped, Maria was twisting her sheets miserably, Cordelia was examining the books that lay about the room, but Helena was for once intent upon her own interests.

"It is the most delightful view I have ever seen," she said with enthusiasm. "It was a very good idea of yours, Cordelia. I have been walking around the garden and I have found the perfect spot for painting, in the shade of the hedge and yet taking in the garden, the wall, and the hills. I wonder if Mr. Burghclere would object to my painting it."

"I am perfectly sure he would," said Cordelia coldly. "You would be invading his privacy. And just now we appear to be invading Miss Henniker-Hadden's. Come, Helena, we must go."

Cordelia's coldness only made Maria more miserable when she was left alone. She did want Cordelia to like her—more than anybody she had ever known, she wanted her as a friend. But she was so alarming with her grand manner, and Maria knew she could no more resist doing what Cordelia told her to do than a mouse could resist a cobra. If only Cordelia could be content to sit with her and not scramble off on these wildcat expeditions that must lead only to disaster! It was all so unfair.

But it seemed as though the gods were not going to allow Cordelia to have it her own way after all. Mr. Burghclere came to Maria the next day with a letter in his hand. Helena had written to him asking if she might paint the view from his garden in the afternoons. "I am afraid it may take several afternoons, for I am a slow worker," she had said.

Mr. Burghclere had no objection. He was amazed and charmed that the villa could have held two visitors the day before without his seclusion or his privacy in the library being in the least disturbed.

"How fortunate that the view Lady Helena wishes to paint is not on the library side of the villa," he said enthusiastically. Then he looked rather self-conscious. "Unless it disturbs you, my dear Maria."

"Oh, not at all, thank you." Maria's polite tones showed nothing of her triumph and elation. Her difficulties were over. How could Cordelia possibly drag her over the garden wall if Helena was sitting in the garden all afternoon, painting the view?

15

Hoist with Her Own Petard

The phrase "hoist with her own petard" came into Maria's mind more than once that day. Uncle Hadden had used the expression of a fellow scholar who had come to grief (though only in his writings, of course), because the critical methods which he used on the works of other classical scholars had been turned on him. His bomb had blown him up. Cordelia had been deft in chivvying Helena out into the garden so that she could talk to Maria, and now all her schemes would be thwarted just because of that; Helena was going to station herself in the garden every afternoon, a mild but effective watchdog. For the first time in months Maria wanted to laugh, but she needed somebody to laugh with. Harriet would perhaps have done, but by the time the joke was written down and sent all those thousands of miles it would have lost its savor. It was odd how she found herself thinking so warmly of Harriet these days.

She wondered a little apprehensively how Cordelia would meet this new situation. Certainly she would never dare tell her how funny she thought it was. Cordelia did not seem the sort of person who laughed very much in any case, and never at herself. But for the next two days she did not see Cordelia. She was kept to her bedroom, feeling very bored, and then Dr. Manfrini called again. Maria had to endure the plump white hands, the rings, and the smell of eau de cologne, which she decided was unmanly (she was almost certain, too, that he scented his beard). But at the end of his investigations he announced, in French so bad that even Maria winced, that he was satisfied with what he found, the signorina was recovering but that it was necessary to be very prudent. She must sleep much, especially during the afternoon, and she must not be tempted to read romances—they enervated the female brain. At the memory of how Cordelia had already told her all this, Maria wanted to laugh again. But who was there to laugh with?

However, Dr. Manfrini apparently did tell them that Maria might now leave her room, for Battista came in later on and asked whether she wished to sit in the drawing room. True, she tried to persuade her to go back to her bed for a nap after lunch (Dr. Manfrini's instructions again, no doubt), but Maria resisted. She could perfectly well sleep on the chaise longue, she said, and Battista, who seemed to be in a hurry— probably to meet the gardener's boy—gave in.

Maria was thus lying among her cushions, staring out at the garden (she had made Battista leave the glass doors open) when the Italian manservant showed in Helena and Cordelia. Helena carried a sketching block and a paintbox, Cordelia a small easel and a folding stool. Both of them seemed surprised when Maria sat up and greeted them.

"We were told that you were taking an afternoon rest," said Helena when the first courtesies were over. "I hope we haven't disturbed you."

"Dr. Manfrini makes Sophy go to bed," remarked Cordelia. "I am sure you should be there now. Shall we ring for Battista—or has she gone out with the gardener's boy?"

"Really, Cordelia," murmured Helena. "I think we should leave Miss Henniker-Hadden to do as she pleases."

Cordelia looked around the room for a bell rope. "She would be far more comfortable in bed. You know that is the only way we can get Sophy to rest."

"But Sophy's complaint is probably quite different. And, Cordelia, I want you to help me with the easel," urged Helena.

"She might be different, but Dr. Manfrini is the same. However, let us deal with this easel first."

Cordelia picked it up and went out after Helena into the garden, leaving Maria cowering on the sofa and wondering what Cordelia's machinations were now. She watched the easel being set up, the piece of paper being pinned to it, the box of paints opened. Then, when Helena had settled herself on her stool, a large, shady leghorn hat keeping the sun from her eyes, Cordelia came sauntering back.

"Why ever did you let them put you here?" she asked Maria.

Maria shrank back on her cushions. "I don't like being in my bedroom; it makes me feel a prisoner," she mumbled. "Anyway, I'm not ill."

"I know you're not. Dr. Manfrini is very pleased with your progress. He told Battista, who told our maid, Lisabeta. So you are ready for another expedition, but I never thought you would be so foolish as to allow yourself to be put here when you knew Helena was going to be sketching outside in the garden."

"What difference does it make?" said Maria weakly.

"We could have planned an escape from your bedroom. I'd thought it all out. We could hardly go over the wall with Helena there in the garden, but in disguise you could have gone out the front way into our garden, along a secluded path that I know of, and down the steps."

"Disguise!" whispered Maria, too horrified to ask more.

"In one of Sophy's pinafores and her hat you would look quite like her—to anybody in this part of the villa, at any rate. And if you walked out of the front door with me, none of Mr. Burghclere's servants would think of it being you. What my godfather said about boldness is perfectly true; you can do whatever you please so long as you don't look afraid."

Maria knew that never, never, never could she put such advice to the test. All the godfathers in the world might stand by and testify to the wisdom of being bold, but Maria knew that boldness was not for her. However, she did not say anything of this to Cordelia. Instead, feeling light-headed with relief that Helena was preserving her from the perils that Cordelia talked of so calmly, she said in a voice that trembled a little in spite of her efforts to seem matter-of-fact: "We couldn't go out of the drawing room while your sister is only just over there. Why, she easily might want you and come over to fetch you."

"Of course she might. Whereas if you were in your bedroom asleep, she would never dream of going to disturb you."

"But where would you be, then?" Maria asked.

"Out with you in the nearby countryside, of course," said Cordelia with asperity.

"But where would your sister *think* you were?"

"I would not inquire. But both she and Miss Buldino are so decorous themselves that it never occurs to them that anybody could be anything else. They recognize that I am different from the rest of the family, but they think it is only that I like books and being alone. They would never dream that I could *behave* differently."

Maria, looking at Cordelia's determined, pointed face as she sat there with the poise and assurance of somebody ten years older, wondered how anybody who had known her for five minutes could think anything of the sort.

"I sometimes wish that I were not so very different," pursued Cordelia. "I would be much happier if I were somebody like Helena."

Maria, very flattered by the way Cordelia was confiding in her, nevertheless hardly knew how to respond. "I wouldn't like to be the same as girls at school," she ventured.

"School!" said Cordelia dramatically. "The unattainable ideal!"

Maria stared at her uncomprehendingly. She was also rather embarrassed by Cordelia's extravagant way of expressing herself. "Do you mean you would like to go to school?" she said unbelievingly.

"It would be escape from a gilded cage," stated Cordelia. "Besides, it is the gateway to higher education, to equal opportunities for women."

"But the school I was at was like a cage. No, not a

cage, a prison. I ran away from it. If I were still there, I think I'd have"— Maria, infected by Cordelia's extravagance, searched her mind for something she might have done—"I'd have thrown myself over a cliff by now," she finished wildly, disregarding the fact that in the dull little Midland spa where she had experienced three weeks of boarding school life, there was not a cliff within fifty miles.

"One has to choose the right school, of course," stated Cordelia. "Otherwise school life is no better than governess life. But when I think how girls are sitting for examinations and going to universities and getting degrees, and how I'm cut off from it and go on learning answers by heart from Mangnall and Pinnock, just the same as my grandmother and my great-grandmother did, then I want to tear out all my hair. Music, a little drawing, needlework, French—that's all we get. It may suit the others, but it doesn't suit me."

"But wouldn't they send you to school if you asked?" Maria said diffidently. She did not see how anybody could stand up to Cordelia in one of these moods.

"Papa send one of his daughters to school!" Cordelia was scornful. "If I even mentioned it he would send for a doctor, he would be so certain I must be out of my mind. Nobody in his family has ever been contaminated by school."

Maria tried to comfort her. "Well, I'm glad I don't

have to go to school," she stated defiantly. "I've tried it twice. I ran away from the first one, and I was only one day at the other, but it was so horrible that it seemed like a miracle when Mr. Burghclere said I could go to Italy with him instead."

"No, I don't suppose you would like it," said Cordelia scornfully. "But then, you're a recluse like Mr. Burghclere."

This charge took the breath from Maria. It was so unexpected, and so ferocious. "I'm not a recluse," she said weakly.

"Of course you are, lying here pretending to be ill so that you won't have to go out and meet people."

"I like people," protested Maria. "Some people, that is. I liked your sisters."

"You hid behind your sofa so that you need not see me. That's just the sort of thing a real recluse does."

Maria knew she could never explain away that, even to herself. It was something she had done on the impulse of the moment and was best forgotten. "But I do like you and Helena coming to see me." Then she added with a great effort, blushing as she spoke, for it seemed a thing that one did not tell people, "And I do hope you'll come again. I do like talking to you, there's no one to talk to here."

Cordelia did come back. Maria spent the next twenty-four hours feverishly wondering which would be worse, that Cordelia should insist on carrying out her dreadful plan of a disguised escape, or that she would stay away. Lying in the drawing room the following afternoon, Maria bit her nails in her anxiety, and then remembered with shame that a few days earlier she was so reluctant to see Cordelia that she had hidden behind the sofa.

But Cordelia came that afternoon, and for several afternoons on end, and while Helena, shaded by her large hat, sketched diligently by the ilex hedge, the two girls sat and talked. Maria was happy, happier than she had been since she had arrived in Italy. She was even able to appreciate her surroundings a little. She knew she could never think much of the Italian notion of a garden, but the hazy, distant hills, blue and gray in the daytime, dark purple and black when the sun sank behind them, seemed more attractive than they had before, though still woefully unlike England.

It was usually Cordelia who talked, while Maria, admiring, and still amazed that she should be entertaining so exotic a companion, listened with awe. She learned that Cordelia was thrown on her own resources a great deal, since Helena and Miss Buldino were preoccupied with the younger girls, and it was recognized that she had gone beyond Miss Buldino's powers of teaching. At home she spent much of her time in her father's library, and she had been allowed to meet his friends and listen to them talking. But for the last year

she and her sisters had been living in Italy for the sake of
Sophy's health, and she saw her father only in the summer.

"And here I am with pictures and wonderful things
all around, and never a chance to see them," she said
dramatically one day. "Just a quick correct walk with
Miss Buldino around the Uffizi. Her idea of looking at
pictures is letting her eyes rest for one second on every
picture that Baedeker gives two stars to and coming out
as fast as possible. I need to stare at pictures for hours."

"So does Mr. Burghclere," said Maria rather injudi-
ciously. "That's why I hope I'll never have to go out
with him again."

Cordelia was in a fiery mood that day, and she
rounded on Maria. "They've offered to send you to
school, they've offered to show you pictures, and all you
can do is lie there and whine that you don't want to.
People say we spoil Sophy, but I've never known anybody so spoiled as you! Well, there's one picture that
I'm going to see before we leave for home, and nobody
in the world is going to stop me!"

Maria forgot all Cordelia's wounding remarks in her
consternation at this last piece of news. "Are you *leaving* Italy, then?"

"We always go home for the summer, yes. It gets too
hot here. Another week, and we will be back in
Oxfordshire."

"Oxfordshire!" The word made Maria think of green

meadows, of the slow-moving Cherwell fringed with willows, of gray stone buildings, and rooks and bells, and tears came into her eyes. "Do you know what Mr. Burghclere does in the summer?" she asked timidly.

"What an extraordinary pair you are, you two recluses," said Cordelia scornfully. "Do you never speak to each other?" Then, seeing Maria's woebegone expression, she softened. "I expect he spends most of his time here. You can be sure that he can't bear to be far from his books and his engravings."

But the thought of being isolated with Mr. Burghclere at the top of this sun-baked plateau, everything dry, brown, and parched by heat, without the consolation of Cordelia's company, was making Maria gulp dismally into her handkerchief. Cordelia looked at her with a quite kindly expression. "I shall miss you too, you know. There's never been anybody to talk to here before. Now, I tell you what would make a memorable finish to it all. Our maid Lisabeta has told me about a wonderful picture in a village where her uncle lives. We'll both go and see it. Helena has very nearly finished her sketch, and we'll have your garden to ourselves after tomorrow."

Maria was completely taken by surprise. She had thought after these few days when Cordelia had seemed content to sit and talk that all danger of being dragged on madcap expeditions was over. She looked at Cordelia with trembling lips. "But, but . . ." she stammered.

"Now, please don't tell me that Dr. Manfrini says you mustn't, that somebody might find out, that you dare not," said Cordelia impatiently.

She would probably have added more sarcasms had she not been interrupted by footsteps coming over the gravel toward the glass doors of the drawing room, and a moment later Helena appeared.

"Do you know, Cordelia, I have finished my sketch. I can think of nothing more to do to it. I really am quite pleased. I think I have caught the afternoon light quite successfully."

A sudden idea flashed into Maria's mind, and without even stopping to consider it, she leaned forward. "Before you leave Italy, Lady Helena, why don't you make a sketch of this wing of the Villa Gondi, from our garden? Mr. Burghclere says that architecturally it is very interesting." As she said this she was making rapid calculations in her mind. Helena was a slow worker, Cordelia said that, and she had taken six days to make this painting. She could hardly take less than six days to paint the villa, and the Squerryes were to leave for England in a week's time. Surely this way Maria would be saved from Cordelia's mad escapade. She watched Helena's face anxiously, praying that the suggestion would appeal to her. At first Helena wrinkled her large, fair forehead in thought, then her face cleared.

"I think it is a delightful idea. This side of the villa is very interesting, as Mr. Burghclere says, and I have certainly never had a chance to draw it before."

Maria felt a glow of relief spreading through her. She had saved herself. Then she stole a glance at Cordelia. Cordelia's face was savage. In fact the frightened Maria thought that Medusa must have looked very like Cordelia in this mood.

"If Helena comes to draw the villa, I am never entering it again," she announced ferociously.

Helena seemed to be used to Cordelia's moods. "Don't be so absurd, Cordelia," she said lightly, not giving her much attention.

Cordelia turned to Maria. "I warn you, I shall never come here again."

But Maria knew better than Helena. She knew Cordelia meant just what she said. And she knew that she, too, was hoist with her own petard.

16

Monte Albano

$\mathcal{A}$t first Maria weakly hoped that Cordelia would relent, although all her instinct told her that Cordelia was the sort of person who would never go back on her word. Day after day went by, and only Helena appeared in the afternoons, her easel and stool carried through the drawing room and out into the garden by Mr. Burghclere's manservant. Helena would always pause for a moment by the chaise longue and exchange a few courtesies with Maria, never making any reference to Cordelia. Then she would say, "I must not disturb you from your rest any longer," and would go out into the garden, where her easel and stool had already been placed in position.

Maria moped and became increasingly depressed.

What was more, she was becoming so tired of her sofa and the drawing room. She even thought a little wistfully of that square far below in the town, where the fountain trickled and the pigeons strutted and boys jumped up and down the church steps. And the thought that the dreary routine of her life in the Villa Gondi would go on remorselessly, month after month, made her feel like a squirrel in a cage.

One day she even told Mr. Burghclere very humbly that she was ready to start lessons again.

"I think not, my dear Maria," he said lightly, looking up from a book catalogue that he had been consulting. He was very preoccupied with his books and his library these days. "Dr. Manfrini is of the opinion that we must go very carefully. He thinks that you have been overstimulated. He says that the female brain is easily excited, and prolonged rest is necessary in your case."

Truly she was hoist with her own petard. She looked so cast down, so tearful, that even Mr. Burghclere noticed something was amiss, and paused on his way back to his beloved library. "Is there anything wrong, Maria? You are not bored, are you? I can give you plenty to read. Let me see, have you read *The Vicar of Wakefield*? That is a charming tale."

Maria shook her head dismally. "I don't want books, thank you. But what I would like—" She paused.

"Yes?" said Mr. Burghclere in an abstracted way. His

eyes had been caught by something in the catalogue.

"What I would like to do, that is, if she would come, is see Lady Cordelia Squerrye again. They are going back to England at the end of the week, and I would like to say good-bye," said Maria in a great rush.

"See Lady Cordelia? That seems easy enough. I will send over a servant to ask for her. I thought they were here in the afternoons. There was a note from Lady Helena asking if she might go on with her sketching."

"Cordelia doesn't come anymore."

"Very well, then. Write a note and send it by Giuseppe. Nothing easier. And now, if you will excuse me, I must betake myself to the library."

"Oh but . . ." pleaded Maria, aware that Cordelia would never come on a summons from her.

Mr. Burghclere paused, his eyebrows raised. His expression was becoming rather impatient. "Well?"

"Do you think you could possibly write the note? Cordelia is rather an odd girl. She might not come if just I wrote. She might think that you didn't mean her to come, didn't want her," she gabbled.

Mr. Burghclere sighed. "If that is what you wish, I will write. Now, I really must get back to my books." And with that Maria had to be content. She did not feel very much cheered. After all, supposing Mr. Burghclere did remember to write, it was very uncertain that Cordelia would taken any notice.

But Cordelia came. The next afternoon she was there, walking behind Helena with the easel and the stool. But her face was so cold and remote that Maria's heart almost failed her. It would have been better to have left Cordelia alone than to entertain her in her Medusa mood. Cordelia settled her sister outside and then came in. She stood over the sofa like an avenging Fury, and Maria quailed.

"Well, you were afraid to ask yourself, so you made Mr. Burghclere write. What do you want?"

Maria hardly knew what she wanted. But the first need was somehow to soothe Cordelia. "I'll do anything you want. I'll go out and see the picture with you. I'm sorry about asking your sister to come," she blurted out, staring piteously up at Cordelia.

"Do you think I want to go dragging you like a millstone behind me? It was bad enough having you moaning and wailing all the time we were in town. You don't think *I* enjoy having you with me, do you? It is only that one doesn't go out by oneself, and you seemed to be the only possible person to take. However, I *shall* go by myself. Tomorrow."

"Then do take me too," Maria begged abjectly. "I won't be silly this time, I really won't. Only I won't see you again for months and months. Never, perhaps." Two fat tears rolled down her cheeks.

"What is the good?" Cordelia's voice, however, was

softer. "You have put a stop to all that yourself by asking Helena to sit there all afternoon."

"You could think of some way to tell her not to come," quavered Maria. "You're so good at thinking of plans, of making people do things. And I could go to my bedroom again."

"Go back to your bedroom by all means. But I am not sure that the disguise plan will do. You would have to go through our garden, and everybody would be very alarmed if they thought they saw somebody looking like Sophy out in the afternoon. No, we must think of something else." But Cordelia's manner was growing less stiff. She looked into the garden thoughtfully, and then strode out. Maria could hear her exclaiming outside.

"That's really very nice, Helena. You mustn't put another stroke on it. No, I know that it looks a little unfinished, but that adds so much to its charm. Like those Impressionist pictures that we saw in the Salon in Paris this year. Do you remember Monsieur Cézanne's landscapes? No, I know you didn't care for them, but I did. I am not going to allow you to put your brush on the paper again. There, now I've got it, and you can't!" And a second later, holding a piece of paper aloft, Cordelia stalked back into the drawing room. She gave a wry smile and made a little face in Maria's direction, and flapped the sketch at her. Behind came Helena, looking a little confused, but flushed and pleased.

"Besides, Helena," pursued Cordelia. "There are only two afternoons left. On one of them we are going into Florence to choose presents to take back to England, and you won't want to spend the last day scrambling at your drawing. The trouble with your sketches is that you never know where to leave off. You go on decorating them as if they were Christmas trees. I have managed to catch this one in time. And I expect Miss Henniker-Hadden is tired by your afternoon visits; no doubt she will spend tomorrow afternoon in her bedroom." She looked at Maria very significantly as she said this, and Maria gave a hesitating smile, and a little nod.

Battista seemed surprised, even alarmed when Maria stated the following afternoon that she wished to rest in her bedroom that day. But Maria had no attention to give to what Battista thought. Her whole mind was preoccupied with the afternoon's expedition, and all she wanted was to get Battista out of the room as soon as she could. She had achieved this, and was sitting on the floor, worrying about what boots she should wear, when there was a light rap on the shutters outside. Maria flew across the room in her stockinged feet and threw the shutters back. Cordelia was standing outside. She pulled herself up on to the window ledge and dropped down inside.

"I can't decide what boots to wear, my thin ones

or my thick ones," Maria said breathlessly.

"Well, as far as I can make out, it will be a rough road, but on the other hand, it will be hot. So you must please yourself." Cordelia was staring at the bed in a thoughtful way. "We must put your bolster down inside the bedclothes so that your maid will think you are still sleeping. The shutters make the room very dark, so it will probably deceive her. That's why I told you to be in your bedroom. The place where we're going is quite far and we'll probably be rather late back."

"But how have you managed with your governess and your sisters?" Maria asked timidly.

"They've gone to Florence to buy presents to take home. I said I would stay, as you wanted to see me. Miss Buldino and Helena decided that for once it didn't matter about Sophy's sleep. She never sleeps anyway, she's always pattering around the room, looking at herself in the glass and trying to imagine herself as a storybook heroine. And I told them so. I'm safe till six o'clock. The train from Florence doesn't get in until half past five."

They started out, as they had on the previous occasion, by crossing the garden, scrambling along the wall, going the length of the Squerryes' garden, and down the steps. But they did not follow the dusty white road down into the town. Instead, Cordelia, with a preoccupied look, went up the road a little way in the direction of the villa. Then she saw what she wanted, a road even

smaller and dustier than the other, which turned off it a
few yards ahead.

"I suppose this is the road Lisabeta meant," said
Cordelia. "Of course I couldn't ask too many questions,
she would have thought it odd. The trouble is that it
will take such a long time to discover whether we are on
the right road or not."

As they plodded on under the blazing sun, Maria
wondered ruefully at what point Cordelia would be satisfied that they had taken the right direction. But she
was determined that she would neither complain nor
ask anxious questions. The road wound on through the
hills. The villa on its plateau, the little town that lay on
the slopes below, had long since disappeared. There
was nothing to be seen but the purply-blue hills around
them, and, on either side of the road, strips of green
blades of wheat alternating with rows of olive trees or
vines. And ahead of them the white dusty road curled
like a ribbon, climbing up and up. Sometimes they saw
a farmhouse by the side of the road, where the clucking
of poultry and the calls of unseen children broke the
silence of the hot afternoon. Sometimes there would be
an old man in a sun-burnt straw hat working in the
fields who would raise his head and look at them in an
incurious way. But otherwise they seemed to have the
countryside entirely to themselves.

The road had become much rougher and stonier, and

there were deep ruts in it that made Maria glad she had decided in the end in favor of her thick-soled boots. She had seen nothing so far that Cordelia could possibly be making her goal, and she wondered, more anxiously now, whether Cordelia knew yet that she was on the right road. Then Cordelia gave an exclamation and pointed into the hills.

"There's the village that Lisabeta meant, I'm sure. Up there on the top of the hill. She said it was on a hill."

Maria shaded her eyes and looked. Against the skyline there was certainly a cluster of buildings, but her heart sank at the distance they had to cover before they got there. Cordelia, however, stepped out with renewed vigor.

For the first time Maria, who had plodded behind Cordelia in silence the whole way, dreading to make her angry, ventured on a question. "Where are we going exactly?"

"It's impossible to be exact, because I have only Lisabeta's vague description to go on, but she talked about a wonderful painting in a village called Monte Albano. She *said* it was by Piero della Francesca and that last year a rich American came here to try to buy it. I don't know whether she's right, she may be quite mistaken, but I would go miles on the chance of seeing a Piero. Though now that I think of it, the fact that someone like Lisabeta knows his name at all must mean there is something in the story. Her uncle lives in Monte Albano."

Maria, who did not know the name Piero della Francesca, was deeply impressed by the familiar way that Cordelia was able to talk of him, and began to wish that she had taken in a little more of what she had seen in Venice. She remembered the names Bellini and Tintoretto, but she would never dare use them.

The road was climbing steadily uphill now, and the little town could be clearly seen. It seemed to cling precariously to the top of the heights above them, cut out of the rocks and the crags themselves. Maria, peering up at it apprehensively, thought that it looked like some vast, fortified place built not to house people, but to keep the enemy out. The huge rocks, or perhaps they were walls, she could not tell, rose perpendicular from the hill. There were no windows to be seen, nothing to show that people lived inside. Monte Albano did not look like the sort of place that welcomed strangers.

The road zigzagged up the last steep stretches of the hill, and all the time the vast blind walls frowned down at them threateningly as they climbed wearily with aching legs. To go into the town was like going into a fortress; the road passed under an archway in the walls, into the unknown depths beyond. If Cordelia had any fears about entering the town, about being swallowed up by that menacing archway, she did not show them. She strode boldly on, and Maria trotted, panting, behind her.

Once under the archway they found themselves in a steep and narrow cobbled street where the houses rose high and dark on either side. To Maria it seemed as though they ought not to be there at all. She felt like a trespasser, an intruder. There were very few people about. Once they came upon a small child who stared for a second, gave a shriek, and fled. But Maria was conscious of being watched. There seemed to be people observing them around the corners of windows and dark doorways, and although in her nervousness she did not look directly down the mouths of the dark entries that they passed, she was sure that she could see out of the corner of her eye people lurking there, watching. Even Cordelia seemed to hasten her step a little as they climbed up the street.

"I'm sure the picture must be in the church," she explained breathlessly. "And the church can't be down here. It must be in the middle of the town somewhere."

In a moment more they had emerged in a sunlit open space. Here, sure enough, was a church. It looked a very big church for such a small town. Three doors, a large one flanked by two smaller ones, faced into the square. But they were all shut. Cordelia walked quickly over, and she and Maria pushed each of them in turn.

But it was useless, it was like trying to break into the Bank of England. The doors did not even have a latch or a handle to them, there was just a keyhole, and they were quite plainly locked. The sound of tittering behind them made them turn swiftly. There was a group of four or five boys watching them, brown-legged boys with cropped heads and faded overalls.

Cordelia spoke to them in Italian in imperious tones. Maria understood her to say that she wished to go into the church and desired to know why it was not open.

The boys made no effort to move. They looked at one another and sniggered.

"Why is it not open?" persisted Cordelia angrily.

One of the boys stepped forward and said something in rapid Italian, then dived back into the group again as though he were afraid Cordelia might strike him.

"What's wrong?" said Maria desperately. She could understand Cordelia's Italian, but not the boy's, and she was afraid he was saying that she and Cordelia had no right to be there at all.

"He says it is the hour of the siesta," said Cordelia curtly. She was fumbling in her pocket for something, and with an air of relief pulled out a few small coins. The boys watched avidly as she held out her hand. "Fetch the key," she commanded.

The boy who had spoken before darted forward, snatched the money, and went running off. Cordelia and Maria were left standing there uneasily on the steps. If this was the main square of the town, it was a poor place. All it consisted of was a cluster of impenetrably shuttered houses with paint so baked and blistered that it had long since lost its color, and stucco that had peeled off in great scabs. There was one small shop that might be a wineshop, and the girls could see a cluster of shadows that seemed to be standing just inside the door, watching.

The boy was back again with the key very quickly. He fitted it into one of the smaller doors, turned it, and held the door open. Cordelia and Maria pushed their way past a leather curtain and stood inside. It was very dark, and very cold after the heat outside. The only light seemed to come from the patch of sunlight by the door they had just entered, and dimly from a window covered with a yellow blind, high up behind the altar. The girls advanced on tiptoe up the marble floor of a side aisle, peering around them as they went. There were a number of little chapels here, some with candles burning in front of them; but little as she knew about painting, and in spite of the bad light, Maria could tell there was no great painting here. In fact, there was nothing much in the way of paintings at all. Most of the altars had brightly painted plaster statues on them, and massive candlesticks and dusty artificial flowers. They went up to the high altar, and down the length of chapels on the other side.

"We'll have to ask," said Cordelia at last. "If it's very

precious, they might have put it in the sacristy. Sometimes they do put pictures in the sacristy. Anyway, even
if we did find it, we would have to ask for more light to
see it by."

Maria said nothing, but she wondered just who
Cordelia proposed to ask for more light. They shoul-
dered their way past the leather curtain that hung over
the door and out into the bright hot sun. Then Maria
recoiled and drew back, terrified, against the hot wood
of the door. For the group of boys had now been joined
by a crowd of men who were staring up at the steps of
the church in what seemed a very threatening way.
They lounged with their hands in their pockets, brown-
skinned men with curling black mustaches and straw
hats tipped on the backs of their heads, and stared
implacably at the two girls. If Cordelia was frightened,
she did not show it. With her head held high she
advanced down the steps of the church.

"Where is the painting by Piero della Francesca?" she
asked in her high, clear voice. "We wish to see it."

The men looked at one another and shrugged in a
way that implied they thought Cordelia was a mad-
woman. Maria became panic-stricken. She ran down
the steps and tugged at Cordelia's arm.

"Don't let's bother. I'm sure it can't be here. Let's go,
they don't like us being in their church."

Cordelia shook her off. "We've come all this way. I'm

not going without it. Anybody can go into a church."
Then she raised her voice again and addressed the
group. "There is a painting by Piero della Francesca in
Monte Albano. Can you please tell me where it is? Is
there another church here?"

The men's appearance suddenly seemed to become
more threatening. One of them shouted at Cordelia
and stamped his foot, and made an angry gesture. Maria
did not understand what he said, but she knew perfectly
well what it meant. He was telling them to go at once.
She could contain herself no longer. She grabbed Cordelia's hand, tugged her with a strength she did not know
she had, and went running across the square in the direction of the little street by which they had come. Pulling
Cordelia after her, she ran like a wild thing, her breath
coming in sobbing gasps, fearful that ambushers would
leap out at her from every doorway and side street.

"Let go," panted Cordelia at last. "You're pulling my
arm off. They wouldn't have hurt us. Really, you must
be out of your mind to go rushing off like that. Now
they'll think we've done something dreadful." She
managed to tug herself free and slow down. "I wish I had
never allowed you to come. You've spoiled everything."

"But they *hated* us," said Maria, sobbing. "You could
see that from their faces. They might have—they might
have killed us. Listen, there's someone coming now!
Oh, Cordelia, run!"

Around the corner of the cobbled street, footsteps were certainly hurrying toward them. But nothing, it seemed, was going to make Cordelia run. While Maria cowered back against the wall, Cordelia turned and waited squarely in the middle of the street. A moment later, and the boy who had brought them the key came flying around the corner. "*Ah, signorina,*" he said breathlessly to Cordelia, then followed a spate of Italian that Maria could not possibly follow, accompanied by much pointing and gesticulation. But she did mark the words "Piero della Francesca."

What he said evidently pleased and interested Cordelia, for she listened intently. "*Grazie,*" she said at the end, "*molte grazie.*" And she took the boy's hand and shook it.

"He has told me where the picture is," she said to Maria. "It's not up here at all, it's in a cemetery chapel at the bottom of the hill. I know where it is. I remember the walls of the cemetery. There was a path with some cypresses leading up to it." She strode on, and Maria weakly followed her.

"But why were they so angry and suspicious?" she said imploringly. She wanted Cordelia to agree that there had been good reason to run away.

"They probably thought we wanted to steal their Piero. Lisabeta said the town had been very angry when the rich American tried to buy it from them."

"They need not have been so horrible," persisted Maria stubbornly.

Cordelia gave a weary sigh. "I suppose this will make you all the more certain that every Italian is bad."

"I didn't say they were bad." Maria was hot and tired and her fright had made her angry. "I just meant they were unfriendly. Like the whole town felt."

"These people were worried about their picture, I suppose. Most Italians are very friendly. Can you imagine any English people caring so much about a picture? I expect there's hardly an English person who has even *heard* of Piero. I think it's wonderful they should care so much."

Maria was silenced; she herself had never heard of Piero until that afternoon. Her relief when they finally passed under the arch out of the town was enormous. Ahead of them the white road curled down the hill and stretched through the open countryside, empty of people. But then Maria remembered there was an ordeal still ahead of them.

"Are you really going to the cemetery?" she asked, frightened.

"Of course. There is no need for you to come if you don't choose."

"But if they don't like us asking about the picture up in the town, won't they be even more angry when we get to the real place?"

But Cordelia would say nothing, and Maria dared say no more. There was no difficulty about finding the cemetery. All the way down the road they could see it lying below them, white walls, dark green cypresses, and the glint of what must be tombstones. At the bottom of the hill they found a narrow, grass-grown track that led to the white walls, and to the little building that must be the chapel. They had to pass a tumbledown house on the way, and Maria looked at it apprehensively, wondering if ambushers would leap from it and attack them. But there was no sign of life, only a few fowls clucking and scratching in the bare earth in front of the house.

The chapel, of course, was shut. Maria gave a sigh that was almost a sob, and sank down on the hot stones of the steps that led up to it.

"Can't we go home now?" she begged.

Cordelia took no notice. "The caretaker or gravedigger or whoever he is must live in that cottage we passed. I'm going to ask there."

Maria watched Cordelia walk purposefully down the track, and knew she had not the strength to follow her. But the sun was very hot, so she wriggled herself back over the stone until she was in such shade as the chapel gave. She leaned back against the walls and was wearily poking back untidy strands of hair from her forehead when she became conscious of a movement beside her. Startled, she turned around. There, a few yards away, stood a small barefoot boy staring at her intently. Even Maria could not be frightened of a child that size. Besides, he did not look hostile, just curious.

He must have been five or six, and handsome in a way that Maria could never have believed possible in real life. He looked more like a painting. He had large black eyes with long lashes, black hair that curled over his forehead, and clear-cut features, very different from the usual blobs of faces that you saw on people in the street. In fact, he might have been a young prince except for his torn and outgrown clothes and his bare feet. The presence of Maria did not seem to abash him or surprise him in the least. He climbed up the steps and squatted beside her. Then he unclenched a fist.

"*Ecco!*" he said proudly. On his palm crouched a very small mouse. Maria was not alarmed when she saw it huddled in the child's hand, half suffocated, but only sorry for it.

"Ah, *poverino!*" she said, using the expression that Anna the cook in Venice had used to her when she had seen Maria coming in drenched yet again from the rain. She took the mouse from the child's outstretched hand and stroked the fur of its back with a finger. The mouse must have needed only a little air to recover, for a second later it made an enormous bound off her hand, landed apparently unharmed on the steps, and scuttled away. Aghast, Maria looked at the little boy. Would he mind very much that she had lost his mouse?

But after the first shock of the mouse's leap he had begun to laugh. He laughed until he had to sit down on the stones beside Maria, his legs stretched out in front of him, tears running down his face. "*Che salto!*" he kept saying, making a sweeping arch with his arm to demonstrate the mouse's jump. And after a while Maria began to laugh too.

They laughed for a long time, sitting there in the hot sunshine, then the child jumped up and tugged at Maria's hand and said something to her that she could not understand. But she realized that he wanted her to follow him, so she clattered down the steps after him. With his head turned back over his shoulder to look at her, he pushed the massive iron gate in the white wall beside the chapel, and leaned back against it while she passed through. It led, of course, into the cemetery, and Maria stood there, rather at a loss. Her first impression was of dazzling white marble, like white icing. There were white marble slabs, and statues, and crosses, and paths bordered by little box hedges ran between them. And around the edge of the cemetery, which was really quite small, were tiers of white marble where people seemed to have been buried in what she could think of only as huge chests of drawers; there were the inscriptions on slabs one above the other, five or six deep, all the way around the wall. The little boy seized Maria's hand and led her to the far end. There he squatted on the gravel path and pointed to a slab in the ground. This was a very elaborate grave with white artificial flowers under a small glass dome, a long inscription, and a canopy of ironwork over it all to protect the grave from the weather. There were two faded photographs let into the slab, one of a man, one of a woman. The child pointed to each of them in turn. "*Babbo e Mamma,*" he said, looking up at Maria.

Maria stared back, completely at a loss, not knowing what was expected of her. She had no Italian to say how sorry she was about such a dreadful tragedy. But the child did not seem to think it was a tragedy. He smiled radiantly. "*In cielo!*" he said, pointing up at the sky.

Then Maria made a great effort. "*Babbo e Mamma miei, in cielo altresi,*" she said in what she knew was hopelessly bad Italian.

"Ah," said the little boy with what seemed to be profound understanding, and he nodded his head gravely. He seized her hand and laughed as though they were now in some way bound together, and Maria at that moment felt a rush of warmth toward him such as she had not felt for anybody for a very long time. But they were interrupted by the sound of somebody calling. It was Cordelia. Her high-pitched, very English voice sounded grotesquely out of place here among the cypresses and the white marble.

"I'll have to go," said Maria in English. "That's my friend calling me." She hurried back to the chapel steps. There was Cordelia, looking angry, the chapel door still firmly closed behind her.

"Where in the world have you been?" she demanded.

"I'm sorry," said Maria humbly. "I went to look at some of the graves. Have you got the key?"

"No," said Cordelia shortly. "The house seems to be deserted, and I couldn't find anybody to ask. I suppose we'll have to go."

Maria looked behind her; the child had disappeared. "There's a little boy, he may be in the cemetery. I'll see if he knows." She found him lying on a path, watching something on the ground, it might have been a mouse or a lizard. Not knowing how to call to him or what to say, Maria went up and took him by the hand. He came willingly enough, and she led him to Cordelia. Cordelia looked him up and down. Obviously she thought him too young to be of any use. But she tried nevertheless.

"Can the chapel be opened?" she said in Italian. "We wish to see a picture inside."

The child seemed to understand perfectly. "Ah," he said, "*Il Piero della Francesca!*" Then he said a lot more, and went running off.

Cordelia looked after him triumphantly. "He says he's going to fetch the key. He can't ask his grandfather because his grandfather is away for the day, but he knows where the key is kept."

The child was soon back with an enormous key which he put into the lock. Then he pushed open the door and stood back triumphantly. "*Ecco! Piero della Francesca,*" he said with great reverence. "*Bellissimo!*"

Light flooded the chapel and the picture that stood above the altar. It was a tiny chapel with great mildewy patches of damp on the ceiling and on the crumbling plaster of the walls. All that it contained were a few cane-bottomed chairs with the seats dropping out of them, the altar, and the picture above it. But the picture was wonderful. Maria accepted that as soon as her eyes rested on it. It was a painting of a figure of a female saint who held her mantle wide to shelter small figures of men and women kneeling below its folds with uplifted faces. There was something about the brooding, withdrawn expression on the face of the saint, and the pale, luminous blue of her robes that made the picture almost heavenly, Maria thought. She sat down in one of the broken-seated chairs and stared at it. She stared at it longer than she had ever in her life looked at a picture. Cordelia sat beside her, looking up at it too. At first Maria heard the little boy on the steps outside, bouncing a marble or a stone monotonously, up and down the steps, but then she forgot about it. Only when Cordelia stirred beside her did she come back to reality.

"It's a very protecting sort of picture," she remarked timidly. "A good picture to look at when you're at a funeral."

"The *Madonna della Misericordia*," said Cordelia. "I don't suppose many other English people besides us have seen it. Well, it's been worth everything to see it. Though I don't suppose you will agree."

"I think it's wonderful." Maria still went on staring. "Are there any other pictures by Piero della Francesca, I mean that I can see?"

"Of course there are. There are two or three in London. There's one in the Uffizi in Florence. But you'll never see them, you hate picture galleries so."

"I don't think I do anymore," said Maria humbly.

Back at the Villa

The way home did not seem very long, surprisingly. They talked no more than they had on the way out, and Maria stared in front of her unseeingly, trying to remember the exact way the folds of robe had fallen from the Virgin's arm, the way her eyelids half veiled her eyes, the wondering expression on the faces of the little figures that sheltered beneath her. She wanted to fix it in her mind's eye forever. And with all this was linked the memory of the little boy, who had really seemed to like her. She had not often felt before that somebody liked her; it made her extraordinarily happy. What was more, she recalled for the first time the happiness of that visit to Torcello many weeks before. After all, she did like Italy.

The shadows were growing long by the time they reached the point where the Monte Albano road met the road down to Feronia, and the sound of a church bell came up to them from the town. Cordelia stiffened.

"Mercy! It must be six o'clock. We've been out for four hours."

Curiously, it was Cordelia who was troubled about the time. Maria felt quite detached from the details of everyday life, her mind still on the picture, the chapel, and the little boy.

"The train from Florence will have arrived a long time ago. They must all be back at the villa by now," Cordelia went on.

"Will they be worrying?" Maria asked.

"They think I am taking tea with you. I certainly hope they haven't sent Lisabeta to fetch me." Cordelia quickened her pace and hurried over the grass to the bottom of the steps. "You seem very calm," she said, glancing over her shoulder at Maria. "I wonder if your maid has discovered the bolster in your bed yet?"

Now that the Villa Gondi was almost in sight, Maria came back to her senses. Six o'clock! Battista usually came in to her soon after five. Whatever would she make of the bolster? She could not fail to notice it, and it made the whole escapade more disreputable. In fact, Maria could hardly believe now what she had done that afternoon. She looked back for a moment down the steps she had already toiled up, and at the red roofs of the little town below. Cordelia and she had been a hundred times farther than that, into unknown, hostile territory. How had they ever found the courage? She marveled as she thought of it.

They did the last lap at a trot and thrust their way in through the gate. Cordelia pushed her hair back, settled her hat straight, and made off for the villa. She looked back over her shoulder.

"I suppose you are bitterly regretting the whole afternoon. I can tell you that whatever happens, *I* am not." And she marched off.

"I'm not," wailed Maria, "but I do hope they didn't find the bolster." Cordelia did not seem to have heard, and Maria, after looking at her retreating back with a desolate feeling of desertion, went running down the path toward the hedge that separated the two gardens. She scrambled up onto the wall, and holding on to the twigs of the hedge inched her way along as she had done before.

She was half aware that there was a faint smell of tobacco smoke in the air, but her mind was on the bolster in her bed, and how she could find out at once whether Battista had been into her room. She jumped down into the garden and found herself on all fours, at the feet of Mr. Burghclere, Dr. Manfrini, and, of all unexpected people, Dr. Jessop.

She was so startled that she could do nothing. She just crouched on the gravel and stared at them, gasping. The shock of it almost hurt. It was like the time when James Smith had bounced out of a cupboard at her in the dark. He had been slippered by his father for that, but nobody could be blamed for this fright except Maria herself. In fact, Mr. Burghclere and Dr. Manfrini seemed as startled as she was. It was Dr. Jessop who rose best to the situation. He stepped forward, helped Maria to her feet, and brushed the gravel off her.

"I am delighted to see you, Maria, my dear. And where have you sprung from? Not from an invalid's sofa, surely?"

Maria had not properly come to her senses yet. She did not attempt any explanation of what she was doing, she just pointed with a trembling hand toward the parapet. "I came over that way," she said, hanging her head, not daring to look at any of them. Dr. Manfrini seemed to be expostulating very rapidly in Italian, and Mr. Burghclere was saying from time to time, "But I do not understand at all. Her maid told me only half an hour ago that she was still in her bedroom asleep."

Still holding Maria by the arm, Dr. Jessop strolled over to the parapet and peered over. He whistled. "Maria, you have a nerve that many a mountaineer would envy. Did you know she went in for this sort of thing, Burghclere?"

"Upon my soul, I did not!" Mr. Burghclere seemed to have difficulty in finding words. "Do you think—is it possible—could she be delirious, sleepwalking, do you think?"

Dr. Jessop pursed his lips and stared hard at Maria. "I shouldn't have said it was sleepwalking myself." Maria, crimson-cheeked, tears starting to her eyes, stared back. "Delirium, now, I wonder? What would you say yourself, Maria?"

But Maria could bear it no longer. Another second, and she knew she would be in tears. She pulled herself free from Dr. Jessop and ran for the villa. She tried to take the last two terrace steps in one stride, but she misjudged the height, caught her toe, and fell heavily. The pain of it made her feel quite sick for a moment, and everything swung mistily in front of her eyes. She could only sit there on top of the steps, hugging her bruised knee.

"And the moral of that is," said Dr. Jessop's voice above her head, "never go up steps two at a time on a hot evening in Italy. Wait for a cool one in England. Do I take it that you wish to go indoors?"

Maria nodded, and allowed herself to be helped once again to her feet and conducted through the glass doors into the drawing room. Then she clutched Dr. Jessop's arm. "I want to go to my room," she said feverishly. "I don't want them to see me."

"You are a little embarrassed by the situation? Very well, we'll go anywhere you say."

Once in the bedroom, Dr. Jessop clucked his tongue at the darkness. He flung back a shutter. "The way these Italians like to shut out the light! I don't know why they don't all live at the bottom of coal mines. Why, bless me, what's this in your bed?" He began to laugh. "The last time I saw a bolster arranged like that was in my own bed thirty years ago. I went out for a midnight picnic with my brother Sam. Not that there was the slightest need for the bolster, but it added to the fun of the thing. Who put you up to that?"

"Does anybody know?" moaned Maria with a feeling that the disgrace of the affair would be infinitely worse if Mr. Burghclere and Dr. Manfrini had been told of the bolster.

"It deceived them all," said Dr. Jessop solemnly. "Your maid said that she had repeatedly been in to see how you were, but you were always sleeping heavily. But who put you up to it? I refuse to credit that a mouse like you is capable of tricks of that sort."

"It was Cordelia," said Maria without thinking.

"And could it be Cordelia that you were visiting when you went on that mountaineering expedition over the wall?"

Maria was scarlet with confusion. "You mustn't tell anybody about Cordelia, about what she does. Her governess and her sisters think she's very good and proper, and it would be terrible if they knew."

"The truth about Cordelia, whoever Cordelia may be. You've certainly roused my curiosity, Maria, my dear. But you needn't worry about my telling anybody. Dr. Manfrini and I arrived only a little while ago on the same train out from Florence, as it happened, and we are quite unable to communicate with each other without a translator. As for your Mr. Burghclere, he doesn't strike me as the sort of man one could possibly chatter to. So your Cordelia's safe."

"But how did you come here? Why did you?" Maria burst out. She was just recovering her senses, and realizing what a wholly unaccountable thing it was to find Dr. Jessop in the gardens of the Villa Gondi.

"Why did I come? Because of you, of course. Your letters to Harriet and the one communication that Mr. Burghclere has deigned to make to me made things sound bad, so out I came. I wrote to Mr. Burghclere to tell him I was on my way, but it seems that he is so immersed in his books these days that half the time he doesn't bother to open his letters. That's why I took you all by surprise. He's a fine person to have charge of a child, I must say," said Dr. Jessop indignantly.

"You came all this way just because of me?" said Maria, wondering. She felt hot with shame and remorse. "How dreadful. Oh, I am so very sorry."

"Now, why should you be sorry?"

"I mean," stammered Maria, afraid that she had sounded as though she did not want to see him, "it's hundreds of miles, and you came because you thought I was ill and I wasn't really, at least not since Venice. Oh, dear." She buried her face in her hands. "You see, it was that I hated seeing pictures and art galleries and things, so I pretended to take a long time getting well. And then everybody started believing that I really was ill. Except Cordelia, and she made me go out with her."

"I came because it sounded as though life in Italy was not suiting you. I've been here only fifteen minutes or so, but I have no reason to change my mind. In fact, I find you in the charge of an incompetent Italian physician who actually seems to scent his beard and a scholar whose mind is on nothing but his books. So I am proposing to take you back to Oxford. What do you say to that?"

"Oh, yes," said Maria fervently, thinking of it as a miraculous deliverance from all her immediate difficulties, from the embarrassment of having to face Mr. Burghclere and Dr. Manfrini.

But even the next day, when she had thought it over, and had been able to speak to Dr. Jessop with a rather clearer head than she had had the day before, she still thought that life in Oxford was to be preferred to life at the villa.

"You see," she said with much embarrassment, "I am turning into a recluse. Cordelia said I was. And I do feel lonely, and Cordelia is going."

"You are *not* a recluse," Dr. Jessop said emphatically, "or you wouldn't feel lonely. And have you got over your horrors about school, now, eh?"

"I suppose it won't be so bad—with you and Harriet to come home to," mumbled Maria. "Cordelia says that school is her unattainable ideal."

"That's the spirit! I don't know about unattainable ideals, but it'll make a world of difference to young Hetty to have you, jolly her up a bit. In fact, it might be the making of both of you, put a bit of spirit into you, make you more like this Cordelia of yours. I don't favor girls' schools that much myself—a collection of finicky old maids, in my opinion—but at least we'll all be able to laugh at them together. And Hetty isn't unhappy at the Oxford Ladies' College, not a bit."

It was amazing how kind Dr. Jessop was. He never pressed for reasons or explanations, and somehow he managed to put matters right with Mr. Burghclere so that Maria never had to account for the way she had posed as an invalid long after she had been well. As for Dr. Manfrini, Maria did not hear a word more about him. No doubt he had driven off in a great state of wrath at the way he had been summoned all the way from Florence to attend a mad English girl.

Mr. Burghclere seemed to be almost light-hearted when Maria saw him the morning after her dramatic leap over the wall. With a jolt she realized that he was probably glad to have her taken off his hands. "I met Miss Buldino today," he said almost jubilantly. "And she tells me that they leave for England tomorrow. I thought you might care to take leave of Lady Helena and Lady Cordelia, so I asked them to call in this afternoon."

Maria did not wish for anything of the sort, but there was nothing to be done about it, and in the end the ordeal was less than she expected. Helena was so very grown-up and easy in her manner, Maria felt safe with her. She allowed Helena to talk to her about their life in Oxfordshire, and watched with the corner of an eye Cordelia and Dr. Jessop, who seemed to be getting on famously. As long as she did not have to talk to Cordelia herself, she was happy. She felt ashamed of her ignoble behavior at Monte Albano the day before, and certain that Cordelia despised her. So she was enormously relieved when the brief visit came to an end without any conversation with Cordelia except formal greetings.

Maria and Dr. Jessop left the Villa Gondi very early the next morning for the long drive to the little station. It lay far below at the bottom of the valley, beyond the town that clustered on the slopes of the hill. Up on the rocky plateau where the villa stood, the sky was a luminous pale blue, like the blue of the dress of Piero's Virgin, but below, the town and the valley were lost in mist. To Maria, peering over the parapet of the still, cool garden for the last time, and sniffing the fresh smell of early summer, it was as if the villa were floating in a sea of clouds. Then, miraculously, as they drove down, the sun pierced the mist, and it cleared in drifts, leaving milky pools here and there in hollows, and above the river that ran through the valley.

As they rattled over the cobbled square of the town the bell was clanging in the bell tower, and one or two women with black shawls pulled over their heads, on their way to the church, shaded their eyes against the bright morning light to look after the carriage. Maria looked around her wistfully.

"I feel I've hardly seen Italy at all," she said sadly. "And I've only just discovered that I like it."

"You'll be back," said Dr. Jessop roundly. "Mr. Burghclere asked specially that you should come back for some months of the year. He's fond of you in his odd way, even though he found the responsibility of an invalid more than he had bargained for."

"Fond of me?" said Maria, astonished. "I didn't think anybody was." Then she remembered the little boy outside the chapel at Monte Albano. "Well, not people who knew me at all."